# HEART
## OF THE
# VILLAIN

# Heart of the Villain
## The Cursed Gods Series
### Book 1.5

**Dany Crooks**

**Heart of the Villain**



ISBN: 978-1-965434-01-7

Developmental & Copy Editing: Katie Wolf

Cover Design: Maria Spada

Map: Ophelia Illustration

Chapter Header & Scene Break Illustration: Marta Riva

*To the little girl in me who never felt good enough.*
*I see you. Your story isn't anything like Marlena's, but there's a piece*
*of you inside her. Thank you for making me a stronger me today.*

*& to the villain who started it all.*
*Show those motherfuckers what you're made of!*

## AUTHOR NOTE & TRIGGER WARNINGS

Heart of the Villain is book 1.5 in the Cursed Gods' Series, but is the prequel to the events in Revenge of the Forgotten and is intended to be read **after** Revenge!

Author's suggested reading order:
Revenge of the Forgotten (Book 1)
Heart of the Villain (Book 1.5, prequel novella)
Vengeance of the Gods (Book 2)
Book 3 — Details coming soon!

You've been warned. Proceed with caution.

Heart of the Villain is a story about what happens when someone lets the darkness in. Themes in this book might be hard for some to read.

**If you wish to see a list of Trigger Warnings,** flip to page 199. If you **do not** wish to read the Trigger Warnings, flip to the next page.

# SPOTIFY PLAYLIST
## (Scan me with your Spotify App)

How Villains Are Made - Madalen Duke

Devil's Worst Nightmare - FJØRA

A Little Wicked - Valerie Broussard

Little Girl Gone - CHINCHILLA

MONSTER - Chandler Leighton

Who's Afraid of Little Old Me? - Taylor Swift

Run For Your Life - K. Flay

DARKSIDE - Neoni

Hands - SM6

you should see me in a crown - Billie Eilish

Arsonist's Lullabye - Hozier

Bang Bang (The Ballad of Amy Fisher - Jessie Murph

Bitter - Chappell Roan

LUNCH - Billie Eilish

Start a War - Klergy, Valerie Broussard

Horns - Bryce Fox

Stop This Song (Love Sick Melody) - Paramore

Hide & seek - Klergy, Mindy Jones

No Rest for the Wicked - Klergy

I Did Something Bad - Taylor Swift

No Good Deed - Wicked (Original Broadway Cast)

COPYCAT - Billie Eilish

Paint The Town Blue - Arcane, Ashnikko

Villain - Neoni

# TOLEVARRE

VISIT WWW.DANYCROOKS.COM
FOR AN INTERACTIVE MAP

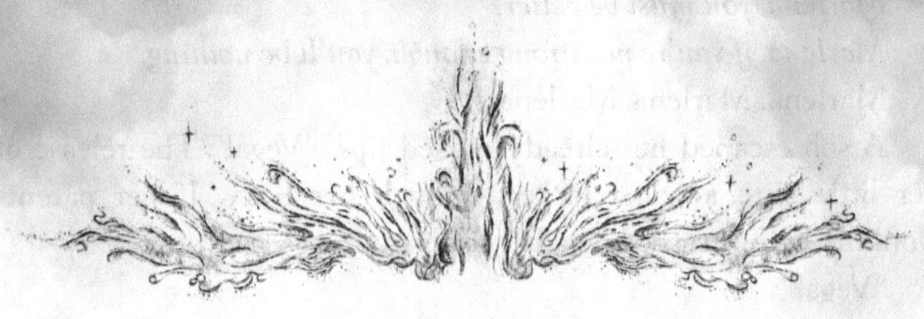

## Nine Years Old

"Mother!" Marlena's tiny fists slammed against the door, over and over and over again until they were sore. "Father?" Her voice quieted.

Marlena swallowed hard, panting from the panic seizing control of her body. She hadn't kept track of how long she'd spent screaming. Spinning on her heels, Marlena let her tear-swollen eyes wander over the small room.

There was nothing but her reflection in the mismatched mirrors covering nearly every inch of wall space. The rest of the room was barren. Not a chair, a bed, blankets. Nothing.

It was just Marlena and the mirrors.

*"You must learn to perfect your craft, Marlena, and this is the way my mother taught me. It's the way I'll teach you."* Her mother's voice rang in her ears as she stared into her vacant eyes in the tallest mirror.

She'd been working so hard. *So hard.*

Marlena would have worked harder if they'd asked her to. She would've done anything not to be locked in this room where all she saw was herself and her flaws.

*Marlena, work on your posture.*

*Marlena, work on your power.*

*Marlena, work on your presence.*

1

*Marlena, you must be better.*

*Marlena, if you're not strong enough, you'll be nothing.*

Marlena. Marlena. Marlena.

A sob escaped her already pursed lips. "Vega!" The release of her little sister's name racked through her body. If her parents wouldn't help her, she knew her sister would!

"Vega!"

Her cries for Vega weren't panicked; they were full of sorrow. Marlena wanted the comfort of the only true friend she had, the sister she would do anything for.

"Vega, please! I'm down here!" She jumped as hard as she could, trying to rattle the mirrors. They stayed frozen against the wall, locked in place, and she finally noticed the reverberation of her voice bouncing around the room with her.

A sound shield. Her parents had the closet-sized room safeguarded from any sound entering or exiting.

Marlena was truly locked away where no one could find her. She fell to the floor and started sobbing again.

*How many more tears do I have left in my body?* she wondered to herself.

Hours passed, maybe days—Marlena was nine, and she couldn't tell the passing of time well—before the sound of a door opening caught her attention. She flung herself up from the floor, and before she could see who was on the other side, it closed again. A small cup of water sat in front of the door.

Marlena scrambled for the water and chugged it down in a few fervent swallows. Her thirst was hardly sated, but it was enough to rid Marlena of the drought in her mouth.

A small part of her wanted to start screaming again, to see if maybe the door opening had weakened the sound shield, but when Marlena opened her mouth to test its strength, nothing but a peep came out.

She tried again, but still, nothing but a quivering breath exited.

Even the sob that shook her body had no noise. Marlena fell to her knees, and the cup skidded across the cold, hard floor until it stopped in the corner.

Sleep came and went, but it was the only constant Marlena had. No food, barely any water, and if she needed to relieve herself, the corner with the cup became the place to do so.

Marlena learned time had no meaning when you were locked up without a way to tell how long had passed.

Eventually, Marlena realized the only way she was going to get out of this room and return to her normal life was by doing what her mother said—perfecting her craft.

Marlena took a long, heavy breath and released it through her nose.

And then she did it a couple more times before scraping her gaze off the floor and forcing herself to meet her eyes in the mirror.

The lights above cast menacing shadows across her face. Her cheeks were hollow, and the bags under her eyes had grown shades darker since the last time she'd looked at herself.

Little Marlena shuddered at her reflection, blinking the image of herself away.

Marlena's ability pulled at the edges of the duplicate in the mirror. Her shoulders disappeared, and then her torso followed. She gritted her teeth and pushed her blanket of invisibility, cloaking her mind. Her face grew red from holding her breath, and her heart thudded against her chest like the sound of a beating drum. *Thump thump thump thump.*

Marlena let go of the hold she had on her invisibility, and her full body reappeared in the mirror. Her lungs swelled with her inhale. The strain on her young powers weakened her from the lack of rest, food, and her overall mental state.

When she tried again, even less of her body disappeared. Eventually, Marlena was pushing and pulling at any little thread she could feel, and nothing happened.

She went until her body gave out, until there was nothing left inside to give. Marlena collapsed and was asleep before her head cracked against the bare floor.

More water waited for her when she woke.

Marlena shook the cup when she finished drinking, hoping a few more drops would slip out.

She hadn't eaten in days and was starting to feel lethargic, her teeth clattering from lack of body heat. There was still no food being brought in, and she was given such small amounts of water that her body was too dehydrated to get rid of any that was given.

*At least I no longer have to pee in the corner like a street mutt.*

Marlena called out for her parents again, promising in between cries that she would work harder, that she would do better.

No one came.

No one would.

Marlena was on her own.

After she wept out all her tears, surely not helping with her dehydration, Marlena squared her shoulders and honed in on her invisibility. Several attempts later, and she was able to make the lower half of her body disappear.

It wasn't good enough though. *Do better.*

She pushed herself until her body couldn't take it, and she crumpled to the floor like she did after every failed attempt.

Whenever she woke, there was always a small glass of water in the same spot by the door. Each time, Marlena gulped it down and then got back to pushing her abilities past their natural limit.

The loneliness started to fade, but Marlena still couldn't look herself in the eyes. The hope was draining from them, and she couldn't stand to see the new version of herself staring back.

Marlena spun in a slow circle and glanced down at her right hand, where three fingers were still visible.

*Three fingers. That's all I need, and I can get out of here!*

She wrapped herself in her invisibility tighter, squeezing her eyes shut, and drove what little control she had left into the tips of her fingers.

Stars clouded her vision when her eyes popped open, and her body was clammy with sweat, but the three fingers were still as clear as day.

A scream tore through Marlena's chest, and as the sound split her lips in two, her whole body reappeared.

*I'm never going to get out of here* was her last thought before she passed out from exhaustion.

Marlena's stomach roared with hunger, waking her from a fitful sleep. Her eyes landed on her reflection in the mirror, curled up in a ball with her arms wrapped around herself. Her eyes bounced from the girl staring back at her to the floor.

Hollow. Inside and out.

She stretched her muscles, wincing at the pain in her stomach. Marlena wanted to cry again, but what was the point? It wouldn't get her anywhere.

*It won't get me out.*

Slowly, Marlena pulled herself up. The room spun, and nausea rolled her stomach so hard she had to reach out and steady herself.

Marlena might not know how long she'd been locked in here, but she did know if she didn't eat soon, she wouldn't have any energy left to fight... and as soon as the fight went out, it would be over for her. "I don't want to die," she said out loud, and the words sounded like an echo. Her thoughts were muddled, incoherent, and nothing felt real anymore.

Would her parents let her wither away in here for the sake of a power she wasn't supposed to have mastered yet?

It wasn't common for a nine-year-old to have full control over their ability, so why did she have to?

Marlena failed again and again, passing out in between attempts. Her body's stored energy was dwindling, and everything took more effort to accomplish. Breathing hurt, her body ached, and her brain felt like mush. But the longer she stayed in here, the weaker she would get and the harder this would become.

So she pushed forward, determined to get out of here today.

Marlena watched as her body faded in the mirrors, the edges of her vision blurring from exertion. She blinked away the black spots and carried on, repeating to herself, *Be stronger. Failing isn't an option.*

The middle, ring, and pinky finger of her right hand remained visible again, like they were mocking her.

Marlena balled up her fist and squeezed so hard her knuckles popped. She ignored the discomfort flitting through her body, focusing on the only thing that mattered.

Disappearing.

Marlena held strong even though her muscles quaked, begging to stop. She refused to fail this time. Through gritted teeth she screamed, puncturing the skin of her palms with her nails. Blood warmed her closed fists, trickling off her knuckles. A chill shot through her, and when Marlena glanced up from the floor at her reflection, blood dripped from midair like she wasn't there.

Her fingers were gone, and so was the rest of her body.

Marlena pulled in a sharp breath, the sound of her heartbeat pattering in her ears. She didn't move an inch, her nails digging further into her hand as her eyes scanned every mirror for any sign of her body.

There was no trace of Marlena. The only signs she'd ever been there were the droplets of blood littering the floor around her bare feet.

Marlena twirled around slowly, scared if she moved too fast or lost concentration, she'd lose her hold. "I did it." She let out a breath, and with it, her body materialized back into view like she feared.

She cleared the room in a couple shaky steps, ready to test her exit. The door handle didn't turn. Marlena jiggled it harder, shaking the door and its frame.

The noise vibrated through the room, perking Marlena up. The sound shield was gone.

"Mommy! Daddy!" she yelled, banging on the door. "I did it! I did it! I disappeared. Let me out, please! I'm so hungry."

The door swung open, and standing before her was her mother, Ryanna Fugere-Caelum, in all her jaw-dropping beauty. Her long blonde locks wrapped around her head in a tight braid, and her chartreuse eyes scrutinized Marlena, raking up her body. "It took you a lot longer than it should have." Ryanna sighed, pointing to the mirror directly across from her. "One more time."

"Mommy—"

Ryanna interrupted. "'Mommy' is for babies. You are not a baby, Marlena."

"Please, I just want to get out of here. I want food. Vega," Marlena squeaked.

Ryanna reached for the door handle. "If you're not going to show me that you can fully disappear on command, then I guess you need another night alone. You are an original bloodline. You are to be better than the others, stronger. You are not a commoner, and your powers will not be weak like theirs."

Marlena lunged for the door and yanked it back by the handle with what little strength she had left. "No! I'll do it. I can do it."

Ryanna crossed her arms and waited, raising a brow.

Marlena tried until her body couldn't hang on anymore,

spiraling into burnout, and when she awoke this time, she was wrapped in her favorite blanket and no longer on the cold, hard floor of the room with the mirrors.

*It's over. You did it. There's no more torture.*

## Eleven Years Old

THEY CROWDED AROUND THE FIRE, WARMING THEIR COLD hands. Khort turned towards it, shaking his butt too close to the flame.

"Khort!" Vega swatted at him. "You're gonna burn your butt!" The kids all broke into hushed giggles, trying not to draw too much attention to themselves.

They were staying the night at the Feras' Demuto home instead of traveling back to Stella in the snowstorm pounding the mountain path. Their parents were inside the house, finishing their glasses of wine over some important Curia business, and the kids snuck out... despite their parents' warnings.

Arlet laughed so hard she stumbled over the log and landed on her butt in the cold snow.

The rest joined in.

Marlena shushed the others through a fit of giggles she did her best to hide. "If our parents know we're out here, they're going to flip out." She put her pointer finger over her lips.

Khort and Arlet were Vega's friends, according to their parents. *They only tolerate you because of your sister.* But in moments like these, Marlena forgot to believe them.

Khort helped Arlet up, and they scooted closer to the fire when a twig snapped.

"Are you kids telling ghost stories?"

They all spun around at the same time, their eyes as wide as the moon hiding behind the clouds.

Olenor Fera lit up behind the firelight, her green eyes glowing with the reflection of the bonfire. Her dark burgundy hair spilled over her shoulders, and she was wrapped in a much lighter coat than the rest of them. The fire of her dragon form kept her warm enough to avoid heavy clothing.

Khort hadn't shifted yet, but his little sister, Delori, already had a few weeks ago... and things had been tense in the Fera household since then.

Delori had taken her mother's dragon form, and it was pretty rare for both children to get the same gift.

"Sorry, Mom, we were just—"

Olenor held up her hand. "You're not in trouble. All of you, relax."

They collectively took a relieved breath.

"But if you aren't telling the story of Mira Viator, then you're not doing ghost stories right."

Marlena's eyebrows rose, and Arlet beat them to the question they were all wondering. "Who's Mira Viator?"

Olenor looked to Arlet, and then her eyes trailed to the rest of the group as she stepped up to the fire where everyone could see her. "Mira was Fraus's Curia seat holder 209 years ago, and she tried to summon a dead god."

Marlena stayed silent, but Arlet and Vega audibly gasped. Khort watched his mom, his eyes never leaving her face. "What happened to her?"

A small breeze kicked up the embers of their fire, and Olenor watched one sail into the night sky. "They're listening," she whispered, refocusing on the kids as a chill ran down Marlena's spine.

Vega reached out for her hand, and Marlena snatched it up.

"Mira wanted power, more power than the rest of the realm wanted to give her. She tried to assassinate the Dimicos, claiming Fraus-born could run the military better than they could, but she got caught and thrown into the prison under Atrox." The main city of Fortis where the Curia member's and Commander's families lived.

Khort's eyebrows creased. "Why haven't we ever heard of this?" he asked. Khort was less than a full year older than Marlena, but he was still the oldest of their group. If any of them had heard of it, it would have been him.

Olenor met her son's curious gaze. "Because the Curia and a few of their family members are the only ones who know about it, and it isn't something people like to talk about."

Marlena stared into the fire, captivated by the crackling of the log. "How do you know about it?"

"Because I was there," Olenor deadpanned.

Marlena's eyes shot from the popping flame.

"The Curia was readying for her execution, and my father was part of the dragon firing squad." Olenor was the leader of Demuto, having taken over her father's seat when he stepped down. "And yes, 'firing squad' was the literal term at the time. They planned to execute her by dragon fire."

There weren't enough dragons for that type of execution anymore. Their population had been dwindling for centuries.

Arlet crossed her arms over her chest and ran her palms up and down to chase the chill out of her bones.

Khort's jaw dropped.

Laws had changed since then. Executions weren't common anymore, only taking place for the most heinous crimes.

"The night before her execution, Mira's actions were neurotic, and knowing now what happened, it should have been worrisome. She had begun talking to herself, clawed one of her eyes out, and ripped most of her hair out at the root. Everyone chalked it up to her impending death."

Olenor's eyes scanned around the fire again when the wind rolled through the trees with a cold gust. "When they put her on the pedestal where she would die, she dropped to her hands and knees and began chanting in the old tongue. The people who knew it scattered, and those who didn't stayed to see what was happening. My dad and the other dragons had yet to shift, and by the time they did, it was too late. She was trying to summon Mars, the dead god of Fortis-born's bloodline, but the gods don't want to *give* to you... They want to *take*."

Olenor stomped her foot, making everyone but Marlena jump. She was too entranced by the story.

"A power like none of us had ever seen shifted the ground, and in the blink of an eye, Mira was gone, sucked into oblivion like she'd been slurped through a straw." She mimicked the sound with a pop. "One might have thought she never existed in the first place if it weren't for her still-beating heart left behind."

Arlet gasped, slapping her hand over her mouth.

Olenor leaned in further, the fire casting a shadow over her face. "They say if you're locked away long enough inside the Atrox prison, you can still hear her screaming."

In the distance, a warbled cry shattered through the night sky with a flash of dim light.

This time they all panicked. Vega nearly jumped into Marlena's arms, Khort took off towards the house, and Arlet dropped to the ground, throwing her hands over her head.

Olenor laughed, bending at the waist, and slapped at her knee as a laugh from down deep tore through her.

From the cover of the trees, the Caelums appeared with Khort's dad and Arlet's parents in tow.

Everyone but the children joined in on their laughter.

Arlet peeked from underneath her arm, and Khort peered from the front porch of the large cabin home. Vega climbed off Marlena, still shaking a little.

Marlena stared.

It had been a joke. The wind was her father's. The scream and flash of light had come from Arlet's mother.

Arlet's dad scooped her up, kissing his daughter's forehead. "Arlie, I am so sorry." He laughed a little when Arlet buried her face in his chest. "I told them not to." He looked up at the group with a playful look. "She's going to be sleeping in our bed for a month now. Thanks, everyone."

Marlena's father stepped behind her, gripping her shoulders with a firm squeeze. "We told you kids to go to bed. When we realized you hadn't listened, we decided to have some fun of our own."

Marlena could smell the wine on his breath.

Khort made his way back to the fire, chest puffed. "I wasn't even that scared."

That earned him an eye roll from Marlena.

Arlet's parents waved to everyone as they took a shaking Arlet in for bed.

"So, was the story true?" Marlena asked, still invested in the failed summoning.

Khort's father stomped out the fire with his boot. Carwel was a phoenix shifter, making their entire family basically fireproof.

Ryanna reached for Vega, who took her mother's hand. "One may never know, Marlena, because summoning any of the dead gods is an immediate death sentence."

Her father dug his fingers into her shoulders harder, making Marlena snap her mouth shut and forget the next question she was about to ask. "Now, whose idea was it to come out here?"

All eyes landed on Marlena, who wiggled out of her father's vice grip.

"It was mine," Vega lied, tearing the attention off her guilty sister. "I wanted to watch the fire go out."

It was Marlena who had wanted to watch the flames flicker to nothing and dragged everyone out here.

Ryanna's eyebrows smooshed together. "Hmm, now who does that sound like?" She glanced at Marlena.

"I—" Marlena started.

"No matter," Olenor interrupted. "Off to bed, and don't even think about stopping for a cookie on the way up." She winked as the kids scattered to the house in the distance.

That night as Vega clung to her side in the bed she insisted they share, Marlena fell asleep wondering: *What if Mira got it wrong?*

Even experiencing a
summoning gone wrong from
the outside would be enough to
send one over the edge.

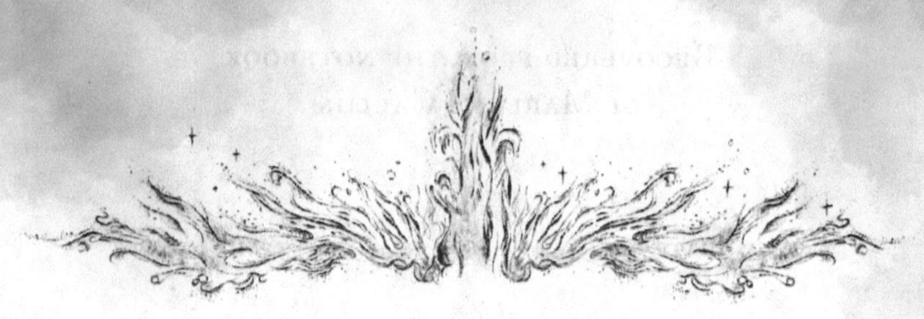

## Thirteen Years Old

Marlena sat at the lunch table alone, her head on a swivel, waiting for Vega to walk through the doors to the dining hall at any second. It wasn't unlike Vega to get stuck in the halls talking to someone, but it was weird Khort and Arlet hadn't made their way in yet.

She chewed on a bite of her sandwich—which tasted a little like cardboard with the worry gnawing its way into Marlena's stomach.

*What if something happened?*

Marlena abandoned her meal, pushing the plate away when she realized her leg was bouncing under the table. She nibbled on her fingernails and tried to ignore her mother's nagging voice in the back of her mind, but it was too loud. *"Marlena, get your hands out of your mouth. People are watching you."*

Her hand shot down to her side like a bolt of Vega's lightning zapped her. Marlena let her eyes wander around the room again, conscious of where people were looking, with Ryanna's voice echoing in her head.

A few classmates walked by, and Marlena couldn't help but eavesdrop on their conversation. "Did you hear she manifested a second ability today during elementals class?"

"What?"

"No way."

"Yes. Professor Cato kept her after class was dismissed."

The girls in matching uniforms passed by quickly, but now that Marlena was aware of the chatter around her, she couldn't drown anything out.

A group of boys walked by. "It was crazy. It felt like more than just wind."

"Yeah, there was a wetness to the air, like a storm was coming."

*Wind? A second ability?*

As far as Marlena knew, she was the only person in Tolevarre that had ever been in control of two powers—it was precisely the reason her parents had been able to convince the other members of the Curia to allow Marlena to be the heir to both of her parents' seats.

She was different. She was strong. She would be the person to change the way their world worked, the way their government ran. Her parents had promised that.

Marlena would be remembered.

The doors to the cafeteria swung open, silencing the room with their thunderous crack against the wall.

Everyone's eyes landed on the source of the commotion.

*Arlet.*

Arlet's panicked eyes locked with Marlena's almost instantly. Her hair was pulled into a tight bun, and a bead of sweat rolled down her temple like she'd run clear across campus without stopping.

Marlena jumped from her chair, forgetting about her bag under the table. She zipped through the students and tables, pushing past whoever was in the way.

"What's wrong?" Marlena asked when Arlet was in earshot.

Arlet's chest rose with a deep inhale. "Vega."

Marlena's stomach dropped out from underneath her, leaving her hollow inside. *No, if something happened to Vega—*

Marlena was too frazzled to speak, stuck inside her own head, where all she could hear was the screaming of her terror.

"Come," Arlet wheezed, grabbing Marlena by the hand and dragging her from the crowded room where they'd become the center of attention.

As they ran, Marlena began to sort through all the scenarios that could have happened...

Did Vega get hurt while practicing skills?

Was she in trouble?

Vega wasn't only her sister—she was her best friend. Marlena would fight, kill, and maim for her. The wind soared through her fingers, the trees of the courtyard leaning from the burst of Marlena's fear.

*"Marlena, control yourself."* Her mother's lessons were always there to remind Marlena when she wasn't acting the way she was supposed to. She wasn't acting like a *leader*, like a *lady*.

Her wind soared high above the buildings of their school, mixing with the natural breeze of Stella's mountains. Marlena felt the wind change, working against her own. It was a sensation she only ever felt when another air-wielder was manipulating at the same time.

It could be any number of students. Air control wasn't uncommon, but there was something *new* about this power. She could feel it in the whispers of the wind.

Marlena ran faster, letting go of Arlet's hand. She didn't look back when Arlet called after her. She didn't slow her pace. She let her wind catch her strides and push her faster, further, until Arlet was too far behind to hear.

The practice field came into view, and in the center stood Vega, surrounded by a crowd. Her dark hair stuck to her sweaty skin, wild and windblown, flowing over her shoulders.

Vega's fingers wiggled, her teeth gritting, and her face turned a shade of red Marlena had only seen when Vega struggled with the control of her lightning—the lightning she'd only just begun to have access to.

The lightning that was no longer her only power.

Marlena inhaled a sharp breath, filling her lungs with a fresh breath of air as she came to a stop outside the circle of faculty surrounding her sister. No one paid attention to Marlena, their eyes still stuck on Vega. It wasn't until Marlena shoved her way through they took notice of her, earning a couple scoldings as they tried to pull her from the training ring.

"Get your hands off me," she growled, her lip curling in the corner. Professor Cato scoffed, reaching for her again, but Marlena was gone, disappearing from everyone's view, not allowing anyone else to lay a hand on her.

Marlena didn't like being touched.

When she reappeared, she stood in front of Vega, her hands resting on her sister's clammy cheeks. "Vega."

Vega's eyes shot open, and Marlena beheld the same eyes she saw when she looked in a mirror. Vega's were filmy, a clear sign of burnout, and her skin felt like a freshly lit flame. Marlena felt the thrum of the electric current under Vega's skin.

"You're burning out. You need to stop." Marlena pushed the hair out of her face. "Take a breath."

Vega listened, her chest rising and falling too quickly.

"Again," Marlena ordered softly.

Wind whipped around them in a fury, scattering leaves across the open field. "Marlena," a voice growled from behind—a voice she knew without having to look.

Marlena hadn't noticed him until now... *but of course he's here. Of course he showed up to see Vega's new ability.* She didn't turn around. She didn't take her focus off Vega. "She's going to hurt herself, Father." Marlena grazed a thumb over Vega's pink cheeks. "Take another breath." Her voice was light as the breeze.

Vega did as she was told and then wrapped her hands around Marlena's wrists for support as she took another few inhales.

"Good," Marlena cooed at the same time Jonan ripped her hands from Vega's face, pushing his eldest daughter back with a gust of his own wind.

Vega stumbled when their hold was broken, stealing the leverage she needed to stay upright. Her knees hit the dirt first, hands flying out to catch herself.

Jonan stood above his daughters but only reached out to help one up. Vega extended her hand, letting him lift her back to her feet.

Marlena watched from the ground as Jonan wrapped his arms around Vega, whispering into her ear loud enough for Marlena to hear. "I am so proud of you, my strong girl. You're spectacular." He pressed a kiss to her temple and pulled her into his side. "Let's get you home so you can rest." He glanced over his shoulder as he turned to leave. "Back to class, Marlena." Jonan glared, and Marlena knew her punishment for interfering today would come later. Horrible images of previous beatings flashed in her head.

Her heart raced from phantom hands wrapping around her neck.

*One day I'll show him just how strong I can be. One day.*

She had yet to pull herself up from the hard ground, watching as Vega hobbled away, using their father's arm for support.

Arlet stepped into view, blocking Vega's and Jonan's exit. She held her hand out. Marlena stared at her open palm, eyes dragging up to meet her soft gaze. "You did what was right. It's why I came to get you. I knew you'd help."

Marlena pushed herself up without Arlet's help, wiping the dirt off her backside. "It's still not good enough." Marlena stored away the hurt, pushing it down deep where no one could find it.

She took the long way back to the dining hall, not ready to paint on a pretty face while the putrid taste of self-doubt crept up her throat.

*Why does Vega get two powers too? Is her lightning not enough? Why can't I have this one thing?*

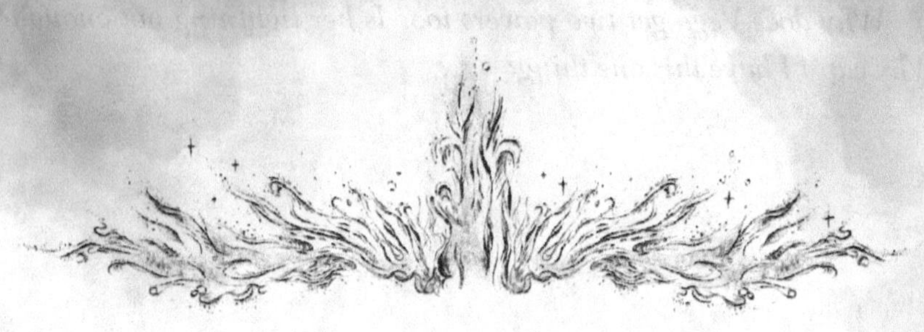

## Fifteen Years Old

A COUGH TORE THROUGH MARLENA'S CHEST, CRACKLING IN HER throat. The force behind it shook the bed, causing Vega to stir and groan beside her.

The Caelum sisters had picked up the flu from school, forcing them to be bedridden for a few days. Vega was finally starting to feel better but still refused to leave Marlena's side.

Marlena had been running a fever all day and had to stomach whatever tinctures their estate's healers thought would help.

Healers could do a lot of things, but sometimes these pesky flu bugs just had to run their course.

Marlena rolled over and thrust the heavy blanket off, swinging her legs over the edge of the bed, and stood on what might as well be legs of a newborn foal. Gripping the nightstand, Marlena steadied herself until the room and her vision stopped spinning.

Vega slept soundlessly, nestled in Marlena's large bed with the covers pulled up to her chin. Marlena tiptoed from the room, catching the time on the clock as she walked on the lightest feet she could.

Her parents and the staff would be in bed, but there wasn't any more medicine on Marlena's bedside, and this cough was going to keep her up all night.

Or worse, wake Vega, who had never been too chipper upon waking up, even without the flu bogging her down.

Taking the stairs delicately, Marlena came to a halting stop when she heard voices much louder than she would've expected at this time of the night echoing down the hallway.

"You have to keep her safe, Ryanna. Promise me you'll keep Arlet safe." Sage Videri's voice was frantic, a sense of urgency in her tone as she continued to beg. "She'll be ready for her seat eventually, but for now, she's safer by not coming with us."

"Sage, you're not making any sense." Ryanna's voice was raspy with sleep like she'd been woken up mid-slumber.

"We've lost control of Vates." Sage's voice trembled, getting clearer the closer Marlena got to the kitchen. "Our people are fleeing. Seers are being hunted for sport. We can't—we can't stay here."

Marlena leaned against the wall, hiding herself in the shadows. Her head hurt and her cheeks were damp with a feverous sweat, but Marlena focused past the pounding in her head.

"You're making a rash decision. We can fix this. No good will come from running, from abandoning your home." The sleepy fog of Ryanna's voice faded.

"Don't teach her how you teach Marlena. She's not cut out for that." Sage didn't listen; she kept vomiting out words as if her personal clock were ticking. "She's soft. A leader by words, not action."

Sage wasn't a seer—she barely had much power of her own. A simple girl from Oro who had been lucky enough to marry into power because Amadeus fell head over heels in love with her, no matter what anyone thought.

"Where are you going?"

As intrigued by the conversation as Marlena was, at the fact that Sage—that anyone—knew what her parents were doing to her,

Marlena's body was still weak, and she was fighting to stay upright every second ticking by.

Sage's sobs tugged at Marlena's heart. She peeked around the corner, doing her best to position herself where she couldn't be seen.

"I can't tell you. I can't risk my other children. My husband." Her husband, the Curia member of Vates—the original bloodline's strongest seer still alive.

The seers had been hunted for years, their predictive abilities seen as bad omens. Dead bodies were washing up on shores across Tolevarre and being found hung in town squares for everyone to see. But more recently, it was the mutilated bodies dumped at family members' doorsteps that had gotten the attention of the realm.

Marlena only knew because she'd heard a few of the Curia members talk of it in passing.

"Sage, take a deep breath. Breathe." Ryanna's words were followed by the inhale of a loud, shaky breath.

"I—I want to make sure she's safe. Please, make sure she's safe. She deserves the happy ending the rest of us can't have."

Out of nowhere, a tickle in Marlena's chest sent her jumping against the wall to hide, a hand shooting over her mouth to cover the cough she couldn't suppress.

It didn't matter if she tried to stay quiet. The mothers in the room adjacent to her had the maternal trait of super-sonic hearing, as well as the hearing of demigods. She was screwed either way.

"Marlena?"

There was no sense in running. Ryanna already knew she was there, eavesdropping on a conversation she had no business being a part of. Marlena rounded the corner slowly, drawing out the inevitable.

Both sets of eyes were on her, trying to gauge how much Marlena heard. Sage's deep auburn skin was splotchy from her blubbered crying, near-black circles marring her under eyes.

Marlena's head spun, but she wasn't so sure it was from her

illness anymore. Her nerves spiked. Unwanted anxiety creeping in that she'd become a target for her mother's anger.

"What are you doing out of bed?" Ryanna asked, breaking the silence.

Marlena's eyes bounced between her mother and Sage, who wiped at the tears rolling down her cheeks and sniffled.

"My cough" was all Marlena could say, and even though it was the truth, Ryanna looked at her daughter like she was a filthy liar.

"Get some honey and sage, throw in a little lavender, and she'll sleep through the night." Sage's gaze fixed on Marlena. "But before you do that, come give me a big hug."

Marlena shuffled her feet against the kitchen floor, afraid to move too fast in fear she would get dizzy again. Sage yanked her into an aggressive hug and kissed the top of her head. When she pulled back, she kept her hands on Marlena's shoulders, holding her at arm's length while peering deep into her eyes. "You take care of my girl, okay? Don't let anything happen to her. The friendship she has with you, your sister, and Khort is all she's going to have left."

"Sage," Ryanna growled, stepping beside them with a small bowl of the herbs Sage had instructed her to prepare. Marlena had been so lost in Sage's embrace she hadn't noticed her mother mixing together her friend's suggestion in a cup of warm water.

Sage let Marlena go, backing away to let Ryanna in. "Drink," she ordered.

Marlena didn't hesitate, willing to do anything if it helped her feel better. When the contents of the cup were gone, Marlena turned to both women and stuck her nose where it didn't belong. "When are you leaving?"

Sage's face fell, and her mouth opened to speak, but Ryanna interrupted. "Bed." Her fingernails dug into Marlena's bicep, escorting her back to the stairs. "You keep your mouth shut about this, do you understand?" Ryanna swiveled Marlena around to meet her eyes dead on, and the look on her face sent a shiver of fear down Marlena's spine.

"Yes," Marlena replied quietly.

"Yes, what?" her mother sneered.

"Yes, Mother. I won't say anything." So scared. Marlena was always so scared.

The sound of a door slamming shut erected Ryanna's spine, and without another word to Marlena, she chased after a friend she never would have spoken to had it not been for her marriage to Amadeus. "Sage, come back!"

Taking her mother's exit as a sign from the gods, Marlena scurried up the stairs and secured herself back in bed, where she was safe from the wrath her mother would birth when she realized Sage had disappeared into the night.

Vega's raspy snore and the lavender lulled Marlena to sleep, but not before thoughts of Arlet's safety clouded Marlena's mind.

*Who would Vega be if she lost her best friend?*

All the air Marlena had been trying to hold in expressed from her lungs in a string of bubbles. Panic rushed through her as she fought against the hold on her head, and her eyes burned from the long water exposure.

Her fingernails dug into the hand holding her in place. Marlena hoped she drew blood as she fought to gain access to the sweet, sweet air only inches above her head. *If only I could do more than draw a little blood.*

Now wasn't the time to listen to the little voice in her head.

All she needed now was some fucking air! Thrashing

uncontrollably wasn't going to help Marlena, but her fight or flight was kicking in, and the urge to inhale got stronger by the second.

Just as she was about to give up, the hand yanked her to the surface. Her first gasp of fresh air felt like an inferno had roared to life inside her lungs.

Marlena hung on the side of the tank's edge, glaring at her father, who had a bored expression on his face—the same look he always wore when he was around Marlena... like she wasn't good enough for his full attention. "That was two minutes under your normal time. You need to create a patch of air. It should be easy, Marlena."

*Fucking asshole.* The thought raced through her oxygen-deprived brain—but the words had to stay safely tucked inside, never allowed to see the light of day.

Marlena coughed up water, despite having fought off the urge to inhale. "I was sick for a whole week. I don't think my lungs are ready for this yet."

"Excuses," Jonan drawled, rolling his eyes and resetting the watch on his wrist. "Go again."

Marlena kept her distance, shaking her head erratically. "I can't."

"You will," he growled, prowling over to her with his hands extended, sending a gust of wind to disturb the calm waters surrounding Marlena. "If you can't learn to control every piece of your power, you'll never amount to anything. You'll never be able to lead when it's time."

Before Jonan could reach Marlena, an alarm rang through the secret training chamber they'd built for Marlena's grueling lessons.

Jonan stilled, his jaw dropping in surprise. The alarm blared softly, quiet and cautious enough that no one outside this room could hear it. Marlena knew it was also sounding off in her parents' office and every other Curia member's private rooms too.

Because this particular siren, the drawn-out beginning followed by five quick beeps, meant a territory's leader pulled their emergency alarm and was looking for immediate backup.

Jonan turned away from Marlena, making for a quick exit while she fought to pull herself together and get out of the torture pool.

She knew what territory had sounded the alarm. "Father, wait!" she called, pushing against the weakness in her muscles.

"Go to your room, Marlena!" he boomed, never looking at her.

She ignored the chill in her bones and rolled her shoulders back, ready to argue. "It's Vates. They've fallen."

Jonan stopped, glancing over his shoulder at Marlena. "Who told you?" he asked through gritted teeth.

"Sage. I heard it from Sage the night she came begging for Mother's help," Marlena spilled.

Footsteps echoed down the hall, and by the sound of the heels, Marlena knew her mother would appear seconds later.

"Let me help," Marlena pleaded on a breath.

"No," Ryanna answered when she appeared at the threshold.

"Pleas—"

"I said no!" her mother interrupted, her screech echoing against the stone walls. "Go home. Lock the doors. We will have guards around the entire estate. Tell Vega nothing." Ryanna turned, ready to end the conversation.

But Marlena wouldn't give up so easily.

"Arlet," she squeaked... which did exactly what she hoped it would do. It stopped her parents from rushing off without her. They both slowly turned to face her, and before she lost her nerve, Marlena continued. "Imagine what losing Arlet would do to Vega."

They would do anything for their youngest daughter—she was their true weakness, and Marlena wasn't opposed to using her against them.

*I'll do anything to have them pay attention.*

Her parents shared a sidelong glance. Jonan raised a brow, and

Ryanna nodded before turning her attention to Marlena. "You have one job and one job only. Find Arlet. Do not get in the way, and if something goes wrong, you leave her. We aren't losing you."

"We've put too much effort into training you," Jonan groaned.

They didn't want her to be careful because Marlena was their daughter, but because they'd invested too much of their precious time into making Marlena the obedient pet she was now.

Marlena ran through the halls of the Videris' burning home, pushing against the smoke with her fresh wind and air. "Arlet!" she screamed, placing her hand on a doorknob so hot it singed her skin.

She pulled back with a hiss, shaking her wrist out to ignore the pain shooting up her arm.

Everyone in Vates was gone. Marlena passed not a single soul on her way in. But Sage had told Marlena to look after Arlet... She'd begged her to watch over the daughter she planned to leave behind.

Arlet was here—she *had* to be. Marlena wouldn't leave without her.

Her parents might not think they were Marlena's friends, might have made Marlena feel like she'd been the tagalong her whole life, but she knew that wasn't the case.

Arlet and Khort were important to her too, just not as important as Vega... but Vega would lay her life down for the two of them, and Marlena would be *fucking damned* if she had to watch Vega lose them.

"Arlet!" she called again, ignoring the heat from the handles as she opened every door she came across in Arlet's family home. "Please, Arlet! Fuck, you have to be alive!" Marlena didn't cry often, had been taught to hold it all in or she would look weak, but right now, she could feel tears threatening to spill out.

*"You take care of my girl, okay? Don't let anything happen to her."* Sage's words reminded Marlena what she was here to do, forcing her to pull herself together and *focus*.

Marlena pushed and pushed, ignoring the burn in her lungs. She bellowed once more, expecting to be met with nothing but the searing flames of the house fire again, but this time, a familiar voice cut through the blaze.

"Mar? Mar!"

"Arlie!" Marlena returned her nickname, listening for another response.

"I'm trapped in my room!" Her voice traveled through the ceiling.

Marlena zipped down the hall, avoiding burning debris as she took the charred steps two at a time. "I'm coming! Hold on! I'm coming!"

Reaching the door, Marlena used all the oxygen she could find in the suffocating fire to break down the door to Arlet's room... and good thing she did, because part of the roof had caved in, and Arlet was left stranded in a burning room with a three-story drop to the hard ground below.

Creating a whirlwind to protect her from the licking flames, Marlena stepped through Arlet's room and yanked Arlet against her with a little too much force. They didn't have enough time for her to be gentle or to think about every move. "I've got you. Don't worry, you're safe."

Marlena didn't know what had happened tonight, but whatever it was, the fear in Arlet's eyes told Marlena that she did... she'd seen it all. "Did you pull the alarm?"

She nodded vigorously, coughing against the rising smoke. "Get me out of here, please. I need air," Arlet gasped, pulling at Marlena's soot-covered clothing.

Marlena's movements felt mechanical as she half-dragged Arlet to the only window in her room. The old frame was stuck on its tracks, melted from the heat of the house fire. Marlena snatched a chair from the corner, shielding Arlet before ramming it through the glass. It shattered to the ground below as a plume of smoke shot through the newly opened window. "Arlet, do you trust me?" She turned to face her.

"Yes," Arlet blurted.

"Then jump." Marlena moved out of her way and shoved her towards the open window with its jagged edges.

"Jump?" she squeaked. Debris fell from the ceiling, clattering around them both as they dodged pieces of Arlet's crumbling home.

"Jump, Arlet! I'll get you down safely! I promise!" Marlena kept shoving her until Arlet finally climbed out of the window, hesitating for too long on the ledge. "Arlet," Marlena choked, running out of her own clean air. "Go! You have to go. I'll burn out soon, and I won't be able to save us!"

With a sharp inhale, Arlet threw herself from the window, and with everything Marlena had left inside, she let her wind catch them both as she flung herself out after Arlet.

Their landing was rough, the ground below breaking their fall harder than Marlena had hoped, but it was better to have the wind knocked out of them than stay a second longer inside the burning home... because a thunderous crack echoed through the night, and Arlet's home started to collapse in on itself moments after they jumped.

Arlet gasped, finally taking in clean air, only to cough until she gagged.

Marlena pulled her in close, shielding her from the sight of her world caving in around her. "It's okay, I'm here. I've got you. I won't let anything happen to you."

Voices sounded in the distance, but Marlena's burnout finally took hold, and her muscles turned to jelly. All she could do was hold on to Arlet's shaking body and remind herself they would be okay.

Marlena chanted the words she'd always wanted to hear for herself...

*I've got you. I've got you. I've got you. You're safe. You're safe. You're safe.*

When connecting with the old gods at a temple in Oro, Latin is the language still used by the priests and priestesses. It is the tongue of our gods. The voice of our people. They won't listen if you aren't willing to connect with who they once were.

SIXTEEN YEARS OLD

STORMS. VEGA CONTROLS STORMS.

Her wind had never felt natural—there was always a wetness to it, an electric shock that traveled up spines when she summoned a brutal gust of warm wind.

Marlena had always known there was something else, something *more.* And last night they figured out exactly what it was.

They stood in the pouring rain over the roaring waters of Lake Mons, just outside their home. Marlena had pushed Vega to sneak out, to test the theory she knew deep down wasn't just a theory—her sister was, and always would be, stronger than her physically.

Vega had gotten powers her parents reminded Marlena she didn't have constantly. Marlena would never be good enough, never be strong enough. Invisibility wouldn't win battles. Wind wouldn't help her lead the people of Aeris and Amora into a new world—into the world her parents dreamed of and had been hanging over her head since before she could remember. They'd been reminding her all her life she probably wouldn't ever be strong enough to rule without them having to hover so she didn't screw everything up.

Last night, after Vega stopped the storm raging over Stella, their parents and the rest of the capital city found out about the new power bubbling within the leaders' youngest daughter.

This morning, a mandatory Curia meeting had been called with

34

all the current leaders and their heirs—heirs including the boys from Ardor and Fortis, who had been hidden away from the rest of the Curia members' kids all their lives.

Marlena had never met them, and frankly, couldn't even think of their names. If she had to point them out in a lineup, she'd never know who to pick.

The boy from Ardor would take over his mother's seat one day. The one from Fortis was rumored to be the strongest warrior their people had ever seen and would one day take over his father's position as commander of Tolevarre's army. If he was anything like his father, the military would continue to be more ruthless than any army in all of their world's history.

"Marlena!" Vega shook her by the shoulders, and Marlena blinked back into reality.

"Were you saying something?" she asked, gripping the sides of the plush chair she was sitting in.

"They're calling you in." Vega nodded her head in the direction of their father's voice bellowing down the decorated hall of the waiting area outside Aeris's Curia meeting room. Pictures of past leaders and their families littered the bright walls, staring at the girls with beady eyes.

Marlena jumped to her feet when her snarled name echoed down to her once again, Jonan's head popping between the double doors. She smoothed her flowing white dress down, holding her head high as she scurried his way.

The vein in the middle of his forehead bulged. He didn't like repeating himself.

"Sorry, I didn't hear you."

His dark brown hair had started to become sprinkled with grays over the last few years—it was normal since he'd started approaching 250 years old. "Obviously," he barked under his breath. "Always stuck inside your head, never paying attention. What, are voices inside there keeping you preoccupied?" He grabbed her by the shoulder and shoved her through the open doors.

*If you only knew.*

Marlena stumbled a couple steps, her heels clicking against the tile. She regained composure quickly, her eyes settling on the long rectangular table full of watchful eyes. Her mother sat at one of the ends, her gaze boring a hole directly through Marlena's forehead.

Jonan's tell was the vein above his eyebrow. Ryanna's was the fake, chipper smile plastered on her face.

*So fake.*

"I apologize for keeping you all waiting," Marlena said with the dip of her head.

She walked with poised purpose to the seat to the right of her mother. Marlena sat gracefully, folding her hands in her lap, and waited for the reason she was here to unfold.

Her eyes wandered down the table.

The Feras sat at the opposite end of the table, closest to her father. Khort's green eyes found hers, and the look behind them made Marlena grow cold with anxiety. Khort was as close to a brother as Marlena would ever get—and one day, he and Vega would bring them even closer through marriage. It had been said since the day Vega was born—she was the only one who continued to ignore any comment made about it like it was some funny joke.

Like she could escape what their parents had planned for her.

His eyes flicked to his hands, his fingers nervously picking at the hem of the tablecloth. His parents didn't stop him, but Marlena wanted to slap his hand away.

*Stop picking,* the voice droned in the back of her mind quietly. It was too loud today, and Marlena was doing all she could to drown it out completely.

"Marlena." Her father's voice pulled her away from fixating on Khort's fingers. "I'm sure you're wondering why you didn't get to come in with the rest of the table."

*Duh.* "Yes, sir," she said instead.

The table was clear of plates, food, and drinks. This was a meeting only—which meant the discussion had been serious.

"You and your sister sneaking out last night should be punished, but instead, it opened up to a deeper conversation about the fate of your future in the Curia." Her father's words didn't cause anyone to react, which meant they already knew what was coming.

Marlena kept her shock to herself, her fingernails digging into her thighs so hard when she glanced down, there were crescent moon blood stains starting to form on her dress.

"The Curia's ultimate goal is to ensure our lineage stays as strong as possible. It's why we still have the twelve original bloodlines. It's why we marry off the children we can to the strongest in someone else's family." He gestured to Khort.

Marlena's eyes wandered to the two faces she'd never seen before sitting side by side at the table across from Khort.

Two boys close to her age from families who'd kept them locked away like lost treasure. One had the skin of both his parents, warm and dark, but his eyes were the color of bright amber. It was almost possible to see the fire he controlled simmering behind his stare.

The other... He didn't even meet her wandering gaze. He stared straight ahead, his jawline like a sharp arrow pointing across the room. His jet-black hair was cut shorter on the sides, the top styled back and away from his face.

He looked nothing like his father, the commander of Tolevarre's army, who sat directly beside him. Lucius's blond hair was the color of sand on a warm beach, his eyes a gray-blue like the Sea of Ros during a storm.

The boy was a spitting image of the Viator line, of his mother sitting adjacent to his father, and his Fraus seat holder uncle across the table.

Marlena knew all the current leaders, had been in rooms like this with them hundreds of times before.

Her focus readjusted to her father, who had stopped talking to watch his daughter's reaction. She wouldn't give him one. Not yet.

"It is unheard of for a second child to take over rule unless a death occurs or the firstborn is unable to take on the task of leading. It has only happened a handful of times, but your mother and I believe that in this circumstance, we have no choice but to make the decision to offer Vega up as the Curia seat holder for Aeris and Amora. She is sent from the gods, hand-chosen with power we've never seen before."

The reality of his words sank in, and Marlena jumped from her chair, sending it flying behind her with a clatter. "No." Desperation settled in, and she lost sense of the composure she was always expected to hold.

Her mother and a few others gasped at her reaction. Marlena hadn't thought about it, acting on impulse rather than thinking it through—typical for her.

"I know the ins and the outs. This is what I've trained my entire life for. I'm strong, and I have fought hard, worked hard for my place here." Marlena eyed her father, ignoring the others in the room like they were the only ones in it.

"Not hard enough." Jonan spoke, metaphorically slicing Marlena's throat.

Ryanna reached out and gripped Marlena's wrist. "Sit. We will put it to a vote as always."

Marlena wiggled out of her mother's touch, eyeing each of the Curia members boldly. "If you listen to my parents, to what they're saying, remember that I got *both* of their powers. Powers they don't seem to think are *too small* or *too weak* when it pertains to them. They aren't too weak to sit at the end of the table during every Curia meeting, pretending to be better than the rest of you." Speaking out against them publicly was risky, but it had to happen. She'd been tormented by them most of her life—she didn't care what they did to her later as punishment. The voting would transpire whether she liked it or not, and if she lost, she'd be forgotten, left behind. Marlena couldn't imagine what her life would look like if she was removed as the ruling heir.

Would they do to Vega what they'd done to her all her life? To prepare her? Would they beat the golden child to make sure she was ready to rule? Or was that saved specifically for the daughter they wished Vega could have been? Marlena couldn't allow her parents to lay a finger on Vega.

"Vega wasn't born to rule. I was, and choosing her would be a mistake." Marlena didn't only look at her parents. She let her eyes wander the room, guaranteeing they knew she was talking to every single leader. "If you choose Vega, you lose a secondary bloodline from the Caelums with *two* abilities, because I will never, *never* marry inside this room. If you think I'm to be demoted to the birthing heir, you've got another thing coming."

*For Vega. I am doing this for her safety.*

Her parents stared at her with stone-cold features, never giving a hint as to what was going on behind their perfectly placed masks.

"You've heard the child's declaration... and now we vote." Fraus's leader, Dacian, spoke up, staring Marlena down like she was a lamb headed to slaughter.

She swallowed the knot in her throat but didn't sink down in her seat like her parents would have wanted. Marlena kept her eyes locked on Dacian's as her father spoke.

"All in favor of allowing Vega to become our heir, raise your hand."

The person beside her raised their hand, jarring her gaze away from Dacian, whose hand stayed put at his side. Her eyes wandered over the people with their hands up, noting the nervous looks on their faces when she locked eyes with them. If they were going to vote against her, they were going to do so by looking her in the eyes.

"Six," her mother said through a breath, her hand returning to her side.

They'd had someone with a distant Vates bloodline stand in for the sake of the vote, and of course, they voted against Marlena—as they'd certainly been told to do.

"All opposed." Her father's usually booming voice had lost some of its confidence.

Six new hands shot up.

"A tie." Ryanna sighed. "Well, Commander Dimico, I guess that's why you're here. To be our tiebreaker."

Marlena held on to a tiny piece of hope. A sliver so thin she already felt as if she'd lost.

Lucius's son watched from the corner of his eye as his father stood.

"I don't understand why you can't give one seat to one daughter and one to another. If that's an option, then—"

"It's not. It's both seats or none, no matter which daughter rules. That is the option we're giving," Jonan barked, putting an end to the commander's train of thought.

Lucius's chest fell, a sigh escaping his lips. "Very well." He turned his attention to Marlena, and it felt like she was filleted open and hung for everyone to see the hidden pieces of herself.

Marlena gripped the side of the table, fighting for support, fighting to show them who she was.

No, she wasn't Vega.

She was worse. A child learning that scorn was worse than any abuse her parents could give her.

Marlena squared her jaw and set her eyes to match Lucius's gaze. "Do you believe I am not of sound mind to rule?"

Lucius smiled, slow and lethal. The kids whose names she couldn't recall had their eyes on her now too. No one in the room moved—not even her parents to scold her for how she was acting.

He closed the distance between them, forcing Marlena to turn her back to the table to keep him in her line of sight. *Keep your eye on what it is you want.*

Lucius was the person standing in between the power she dreamed of.

"I vote..." He paused, sizing Marlena up. "Marlena rules. Vega's too far behind. She's never had a single responsibility in her life, never had a lick of training for what it entails to lead an entire territory, let alone two. Let her marry the dragon and make pretty little babies for the world to fawn over."

And then he turned away, motioning his family out of their seats. Katrin, his doting wife and sister to Dacian, jumped to her feet and stood at his side. Their son rose slowly, eyes flicking to Marlena's before following them out of the room.

That was that. It had been decided.

Marlena would rule.

"Congratulations, Marlena," her mother said from behind her. "You've barely kept your seats, but I hope you realize what you've done." Ryanna's voice was tight, spoken through a clenched jaw. She didn't even attempt to hide the annoyance on her face. "You will always be a pawn. A pretty doll to dress up and parade around while your father and I make the rules."

The room broke into chatter, and Marlena couldn't concentrate on any of it. Gods, she could barely even pay attention to her mother's tyrannical threats.

Lucius picked her. *Why?*

Without asking permission, feeling braver than she should, Marlena sprinted from the room, trailing behind the commander and his family.

"Commander!" Marlena called, but instead of him turning around like she hoped, two of his guards seemed to materialize out of the shadows, barreling towards her. "I just wanted—"

Marlena skidded to a stop when the larger of the guards reached for her, but his hand never met skin.

An iron grip stopped the guard, the commander's son stepping out from behind him. "Get lost," he ordered, and they did without hesitation.

Marlena rubbed her arm where the man's hand would have landed, as if she could feel the pain that should have come.

The boy was her age, give or take a year. He was put together like the rest of the children who grew up in the Curia's wealth. His golden-tan skin almost glowed under the bright natural lighting of the Aeris home. "If you came to ask him why he sided with you, don't bother."

Marlena's eyebrows drew together as she readied herself to ask a question, but the boy didn't give her a chance.

"He doesn't care about you. He cares about pissing off your parents. He voted for you because it was against them." The commander's son stepped back. His black dress ensemble seemed casual compared to the obnoxious garb her mother insisted she dress in. "Don't think he's on your side."

The boy turned to leave, and Marlena couldn't find her words. So instead, she said nothing and watched him walk away.

Lucius might not have picked Marlena for the reason she wanted...

*But he picked me, and I won't waste this second chance.*

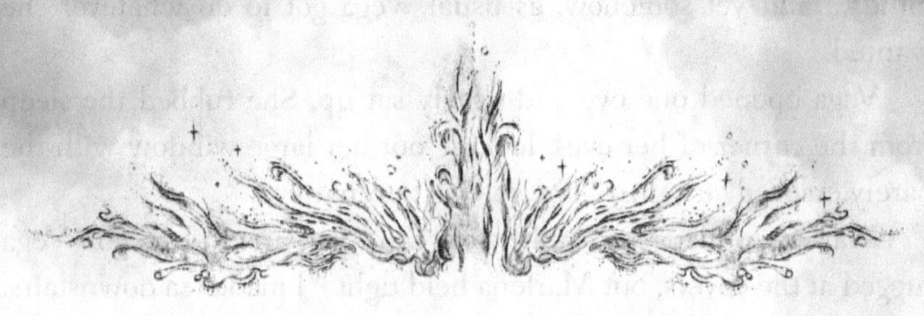

### Seventeen Years Old

"Wake up." Marlena shook her sister, listening to her groan in protest. Vega had never been a morning person, always begging for five more minutes.

"Five more minutes, please."

Marlena rolled her eyes at the expected response but continued to shake her awake. "No, we're going on a trip."

It was the weekend, and usually Marlena and Vega would meet up with Khort, towing Arlet along everywhere now that she was basically part of the family.

When things had gone bad in Vates, they went bad quicker than anyone could have imagined. After Marlena saved Arlet from her burning home, she learned more about what had led up to that very moment.

Arlet had only told the story once and promised Vega, Marlena, and Khort she'd never speak of it again.

Now, Arlet spent her days as a bonus Caelum, doing whatever her best friend Vega did and being kept under careful watch for any sort of power manifestation.

Marlena had been reminded all her life that while she didn't have the extraordinary powers Vega had, she was still an original bloodline, and she was to surround herself with people of like minds... and yet somehow, as usual, Vega got to do whatever she wanted.

Vega opened one eye and slowly sat up. She rubbed the sleep from the corner of her eyes, looking out her large window with the barely cracked curtains. "The sun isn't even up yet."

Marlena pulled her blankets off. "But you are, so let's go." Vega tugged at the covers, but Marlena held tight. "I made tea downstairs. Just how you like it. Get up before our parents do, or *I'll* be in trouble."

Marlena disappeared, stalking through the halls like an invisible ghost. She knew where to step to avoid the old floors from creaking, having spent many years walking this very path to Vega's room.

She had been up for hours, starting her day with a warm bath and some studying. Sleep had never come easy for her—there was always something more important to be doing. Marlena spent a lot of time with her nose stuck in a book. Whether it was studying what her parents had planned for her or about the summonings she'd been obsessed with in private since she was eleven, Marlena was always learning, always trying to get one step ahead.

Vega trudged down the stairs loudly in a pair of tight black pants and a button-up shirt that nearly swallowed her whole. "Is that even your shirt?" Marlena asked, raking her eyes back to hers.

Her sister yawned, grabbing the cup of tea Marlena extended to her. Vega looked down after taking her first sip and raised a brow, as if she hadn't realized what she'd thrown on. "Oh no. It's definitely not." Vega smelled the collar. "It's Khort's."

It was no big secret she and Khort were meant to marry when they were both done with school—hell, the Curia was already talking about it in the open with whomever would listen—but Vega always ignored the whispers like she'd have a real choice when the time came.

Marlena raised a brow and finished her cup of tea. "Did you—"

Vega cut her off. "Gods, no." She shook her head, setting the teacup on the counter next to Marlena's empty one. "We went to the lake on that warm day a couple days ago, and it must've gotten mixed up in my things." Vega didn't wait to grab her riding coat from the closet by the door, and she threw it over her shoulders as a maid came to clean up after them.

Marlena side-eyed the woman, making her sidestep to avoid coming too close.

But Vega smiled, her fingers fluttering in a hello. "How are you this morning?" she asked, buttoning her coat.

The maid, whose name Marlena didn't know, nor did she care to learn, returned Vega's smile. "Wonderful, thank you. And you ladies? Up very early this morning, I see." Though she addressed them both, she didn't dare shoot a glance at Marlena.

Until Marlena snapped, "I don't think that's any of your concern." She worried their trip would get stopped if their parents found out about it. They would find out later, but by then at least they'd already be where they were going and their parents would choose to wait to scold them—they'd punish Marlena, but never would they lay a finger on their *perfect Vega*.

Vega sneered, tossing Marlena's coat at her and closing the closet door. "Down, girl."

Marlena caught the coat before it hit the floor, and instead of dressing in it quickly, she stared at Vega... observing the way she interacted with the help. Vega had always been friendlier with the staff than she had. Marlena grew up with the constant reminder of her status and what would happen if she lost the respect of the others in power. Most of those in power didn't have menial conversations about their day with the staff who worked underneath them.

"Please excuse her. She's snippy until she's had a couple cups of tea." Vega caught Marlena's eye for a split second, her face giving away the words inside her head: *Stop being a bitch.*

"I didn't mean anything by it, only that I usually don't see Vega until afternoon on weekends." The maid began washing the cups and putting them on a rack to dry. "Would you like me to prepare a couple to-go canteens of tea? It's a chilly and wet spring morning out there."

"That would be wonderful. Thank you." Vega reached out and squeezed the maid's hand in thanks. "I don't think I know your name."

"Della."

"It's a pleasure to meet you. Sorry it's taken so long to formally introduce myself. As I'm sure you know, I'm Vega, and the grumpy one is Marlena. She's not as mean as she seems." She flicked her eyes over her shoulder, snarkily smiling at Marlena. "Most of the time."

Slipping into her coat, Marlena rolled her eyes and grabbed the tea from the woman. She didn't say anything to the shifter. She knew she was a shifter by the smell—moss and pine, too earthy to be anything else.

"If we don't get going, we'll never get home before sundown," Marlena said with a stern tone. "Let's wrap this up, shall we?"

Vega waved goodbye to—*what was her name? Delta?*—and followed Marlena out the side door down the path to the stables. "So, am I ever going to find out where we're going?"

Marlena had their horses almost fully tacked and ready to go, another thing she'd had enough time to do while Vega slept soundly this morning. "What if it's a surprise?" She put their canteens in the saddle bags and snagged the reins hanging outside of their horses' stalls.

Rolling her eyes, Vega ran her hand down her dark dappled gray colt's neck, cooing to her young horse.

Marlena's stark white mare with deep blue eyes was older, less energetic, but she was fast and strong—perfect for the few hours they'd be traveling today.

Vega mounted, and Marlena led them out of the barn before any of the staff came in for the start of their day.

Their horses took off at a steady pace, Marlena pushing them to get out of the city square before the sun fully rose over the mountain peaks.

Once they passed the city proper and were on the dirt roads of Aeris's northern territory, they let the horses slow to a walking pace to catch their breath.

"Littera?" Vega asked, letting slack in her reins while she got comfortable in her seat.

"Mm-hmm." Marlena nodded, glancing at her sister.

"You mean to tell me you got me up at the crack of dawn to go study in a library?" Vega asked, annoyance lacing her tone. "We have one of those back home, ya know?"

Chuckling, Marlena stared forward, trying to find the words to tell Vega what she wanted to do. Their world was changing, and Marlena wasn't sure she could stand back and watch an opportunity to prove her parents wrong pass her by when the time came. *You have to be ready.* "Watch the sunrise and shut up," Marlena said with a hint of sarcasm, trying to drown out the whisper of the voice in her head.

Vega grumbled, but the two rode in silence for a while as the sun rose, and they enjoyed the warmth of what was turning out to be a gorgeous spring day.

When the view of Littera's main city's roads became visible, Marlena finally spoke. "Do you remember the story of Mira Viator?"

She'd been building up the courage to bring the tale up for the last hour.

Vega's eyebrows met in the middle, and she scrunched her nose along with it. "Yeah?" She drew out the word. "The story from the campfire?"

"Yes." The next part of her sentence was a whisper. "What if she got the summoning wrong?" Marlena questioned. The only sound for what felt like minutes was the clacking of their horses' hooves against the road.

Vega stared straight ahead, nibbling on the inside of her cheek. "Why would you have been thinking about that?"

Marlena's answer wasn't easy, and she wasn't even sure what she was supposed to say. "Vates falling is just the start. I don't think our realm has seen the last of what's looming in the shadows." The words left her lips before she could think about what she was saying.

Vega turned her head away from the library in the distance. "Everyone only fled for the time being. They'll be back when our parents and the rest of the Curia figure out how to protect the seers."

Marlena slowed her horse to a stop as they approached the large entrance to the Minerva Archives. "Vega, no one is going to help them. Vates is gone for good."

Vega shook her head, bringing her horse to a halt too. "No, they left Arlet to run it when she's ready. They would have taken her with them if they didn't have any hope that she'd be ready to rule one day."

Vega was so gullible. She always believed what their parents told her.

"They left Arlet because she's powerless," Marlena said matter-of-factly. "Her parents couldn't risk being slowed down by her."

Marlena could tell even before Vega spoke that she was going to argue by the way her jaw tightened and her eyebrows pinched together further. "They wouldn't abandon her. They'll be back."

Taking a deep breath, Marlena sighed and hopped off her mare. "But they did abandon her, and no one is coming back, Vega. The seers are gone. They're probably already dead, if I'm being honest. The sooner you accept that, the better off you'll be." She slipped the reins over her horse's head and tied her to a post by a trough of water.

Vega's face blanched. "And what makes you think that?" she asked, staying on her horse.

"Because I've heard it. I hear a lot of things people probably don't want me to." Marlena shouldn't have said that, but it was just Vega... and she could trust her. *Right?* "And because I've seen it."

That caught Vega's attention, her back stiffening further. "So you brought me to Littera. Why?"

Marlena patted her mare's neck and stepped around her, standing underneath Vega's gaze on her tall horse. "Because what if the gods are waiting for the right person... the right people? They might be dead, but their powers aren't. If they're killing those who summon them, the summoners must be asking for the wrong things."

Vega's eyes lit, twinkling with something close to hope. "Could you imagine if we summoned one to fix the problems inside the Curia? We could change the world."

Marlena's smile slowly grew, taking over her face in triumph as Vega slid off her horse and tied him beside Marlena's.

*How far are you willing to go to get what you want?*

It is hard to say what the gods want from the summoner in that final moment before the end. There has never been anyone who's lived to tell the tale of those last few heartbeats.

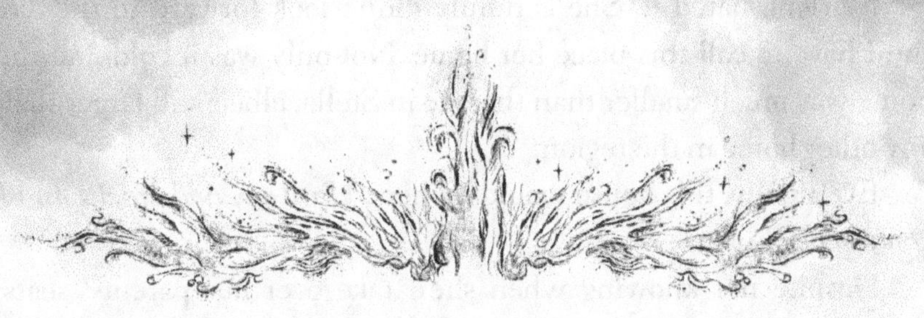

## Eighteen Years Old

Marlena sat in the middle of her plush bed, surrounded by old books and a fluffy white blanket. She'd finished her required schooling this past summer but hadn't been given a break before being thrust into the next part of her life.

Preparing to take over her parents' Curia seats... or pretending to take them over, whatever it was they were *allowing* her to do.

No dates had been set for her succession yet. Her parents were still young, by Tolevarre standards, and she really couldn't imagine either stepping down anytime soon.

*Would be nice to have a little fun while I can.*

Rubbing her eyes, Marlena closed the book and tossed it to the edge of the bed. Her father had given her a week's worth of reading to do in two days, and the words on the pages were starting to look the same.

After a meeting with her mother's council in Amora, the family decided to host a dinner for the leaders and their families. Marlena excused herself early, retiring to her room to start on the work she surely wouldn't finish in time.

Marlena slipped off the bed and into a pair of slippers by her nightstand. There was nothing worse than cold feet, and Amora, no matter the season, was always cold—snow almost always covered the ground.

Marlena hated it. She certainly didn't look forward to the day she'd have to call this place her home. Not only was it cold, but the home was much smaller than the one in Stella, albeit still larger than any other home in the region.

Eventually, this house would be hers. *Until my dad croaks and I can replace him.*

Despite not knowing when she'd take over her parents' seats, Marlena knew it would be her mother who would step down first. Her father would hold on to his piece of control until he was good and ready. And probably even longer just to piss Marlena off.

Marlena ran into no one as she shuffled her way down the stairs and into the kitchen. Most of the small staff had gone home for the night, leaving the place spotless.

After flicking on a light, Marlena dug through the bar cart sitting by the window until she found what she was looking for. In a small glass, she poured herself a couple fingers' worth of the amber liquid from her mother's favorite maker in Imber.

*If nothing else, at least she has good taste in alcohol.*

Marlena licked the excess off her lips as the side door came crashing open, a gust of frozen wind whirling through the room. She jumped, startled by the intrusion.

Laughs rang through the room before Vega, Arlet, and Khort came crashing in on wobbly legs.

"Mar!" Vega squealed, running to her sister and trampling her in a hug. "I definitely thought you were going to be asleep."

Marlena patted her on the shoulder, peeling Vega off while fighting the uncomfortable feeling washing over her from being touched. *She's your sister.*

The smell of booze whacked Marlena in the nose, and it wasn't coming from the fresh glass she'd poured herself. "Are you drunk?"

Arlet giggled, and Khort raised his hands in surrender when Marlena's eyes scanned him over. "I told her she should only have one glass."

"I'm fiiiineeeeee," she promised and smiled as innocently as she could manage. "Look." Vega stood up straight and walked the line in the flooring. She made it to the end and spun in a circle, stumbling only a little. "My shoe stuck," she lied with another fit of giggles to follow.

Marlena put her glass down, sighing. "Let's get you to bed."

Arlet butted in, slipping her arm around Vega's shoulder. "No way. We're all off tomorrow, including you." She pointed at Marlena. "We're going out."

She wasn't off tomorrow. Marlena couldn't remember the last time she'd gotten a break to be a normal girl her age. "I can't."

Khort rolled his eyes, slipping his arm around Marlena's shoulder like Arlet's was draped over Vega's. "Yes, you can. And you are." He tugged her towards the staircase.

She dug her heels into the floor like that would stop Khort from picking her up and carrying her the rest of the way. He flung her over his shoulder, and she pounded on his back. "Put me down, you behemoth!"

He did, in her bedroom, where Vega was already sprawled on the bed, her shoes leaving dirt marks on her blanket.

Arlet rummaged through Marlena's closet, throwing pieces of clothing onto the once-clean floor after she examined them. "Do you not have anything in here that shows off your boobs?" she asked, throwing a turtleneck sweater to the growing pile with her lip snarled in disapproval.

Marlena swatted at Vega's dirty boots on her bed, ignoring Arlet's question. Vega swung her legs to hang them off the side as she sat up. "I cannot go out. I have so much reading to do." She pointed to the books scattered around Vega on the bed, her eyes scanning over the selection from Littera that wasn't on her parents' required reading list. *They can't know.* Her and Vega had never talked about it again after their day of research.

Vega's attention span lasted a whole hour before she was off making friends with one of the archive's students.

Marlena extended her string of invisibility to the books, hiding them from sight—an ability that wasn't common for those with the power of invisibility.

"Mom and Dad are gone for the night. They're staying with Khort's parents up the mountain." Vega nodded towards Khort as if to say, *Ask him.*

"It's true." Khort nodded.

"Ah-ha!" Arlet jumped, nearly having to climb over the pile of clothes she'd ripped from their hangers. She held up a bright red, skintight mini dress. A dress Marlena would never, ever be allowed to wear... but had in the back of her closet for the day she was brave enough to defy her mother's strict dress code.

Khort whistled, barking like a dog—*fucking shifters*—as Vega raced across the room to get a better look.

"Oh my gods!" Vega chirped, emphasizing the last word. "You have to wear this!"

Marlena snatched the dress from them, squishing it against her chest. "Absolutely not!

...was what she had said, and yet somehow now she was dressed and braving the cold to go to a party she didn't want to go to.

Vega was popular—she had friends outside of the two who were always around. Marlena had three.

Despite what her parents might otherwise think.

People their age didn't extend the same kindness to Marlena they did Vega... and she was fine with that. Future leaders couldn't mingle the way others could. But a party where she was certain to not be able to avoid them? *Dreadful.*

They crammed into a small vehicle driven by one of the guards keeping watch over the house while their parents were away. It didn't take much to convince him to drive them and then keep quiet about the whole thing with Vega batting her eyelashes and wiggling her hips like a puma set to pounce.

The party's music could be heard from nearly a block away, and when they pulled up to the sprawling vista home, Marlena noticed a few familiar faces walking up to the home's front door.

"One hour. That's it. Then we're gone," Marlena reminded, meeting each of their gazes as they nodded their agreement.

Everyone scrambled out of the vehicle, leaving Marlena to talk to their guard. "Wait here. We won't be long," she said, and then followed up the stairs.

The music from the band rattled her chest, vibrating the pictures on the wall as they walked into a packed-tight entryway. Vega and Arlet took off towards the kitchen with Khort in tow.

Marlena hung back, taking in her surroundings. She'd never been to a party like this. Any she'd attended were organized events, with ball gowns and a full string quartet—and of course, her parents looming around every corner to keep an eye on Marlena.

A man with a thick beard who smelled like pine and mint came up behind her, laying a hand on her shoulder. "Let me take your coat." He was Amora-born—his beauty unlike anything she'd ever seen.

Marlena hesitated, unsure if she was able to trust the stranger.

"Come on, gorgeous. Don't be shy."

She slipped the coat off one arm, revealing an exposed shoulder in her tiny red dress. Marlena watched as a few heads turned in her direction when the coat came all the way off.

The man hung it up, then winked at her as he disappeared into the crowd of people.

Marlena wandered to the kitchen, where partygoers mingled in groups. In the middle, around the island, were her sister and friends, tipping back what most definitely wasn't their first shot of the night.

Arlet caught her eye, and her smile lit up her face. "Your turn!"

she cried happily, passing Marlena a shot of clear alcohol in a small glass.

"Don't think. For once, just do!" Vega held her own glass up, tapping Marlena's with a *tink*. She threw her head back and downed the liquid, following up with a sour face and a back and forth shake of her head.

Marlena followed suit, but the burn of the alcohol didn't bother her.

She couldn't feel much these days…

The band began playing a song everyone knew, and the room cleared out, leaving the four of them to pour one more.

"To pulling Marlena out of her perfect little bubble." Khort held his arm up, waiting for the rest to join.

Marlena was last to raise her glass, finally caving when Arlet waggled her brows like a tease and said, "Scaredy cat."

They knocked the drink back, and before Marlena could fully set the glass down, Arlet grabbed her by the hand and dragged her to the makeshift dance floor.

Song after song, they danced. With each other, with strangers. A set of silky-smooth arms wrapped around the back of Marlena and slid down the curves accentuated by her dress. The alcohol had taken over, leaving Marlena's head with a new, exciting buzz.

Thoughts of her parents and what would happen if they found out about this party were absent from her mind, and so were the worries she had about the work she wasn't getting done tonight.

Her mind fluttered with the touch of the stranger behind her. Marlena moved her hips in perfect time with the song vibrating through the room, grinding against the warm body behind her.

The voice of the figure who'd turned into her shadow sliced through the haze. "You're so fucking sexy." It was sultry and smoky, her voice full of lust.

Marlena had never felt sexy before—sure, she knew she was

beautiful. Her mother was a descendent of Venus; anyone with the goddess's blood shined brighter than most.

Vega was the one with the dark hair and bright eyes like their father. She was the one who was able to dress how she wanted and be the person she wanted to be. Vega exuded the confidence Marlena had been lacking most of her life.

Reaching behind her with one hand, Marlena slid her fingertips up the woman's leg, her nails trailing up her thigh, where goosebumps began to form. "Tell me again," she said on a breath, continuing to sway to the music.

"The sexiest girl I've ever seen," the woman cooed, her breath warm on her neck as she pulled Marlena's hair over one shoulder. Her lips pressed kisses on the delicate skin, sending a chill down Marlena's spine.

Marlena had never been with anyone before. She'd never had time and hadn't really had the opportunity. Whenever she felt the need to be satisfied, Marlena knew how to take care of herself.

But right now? *Gods,* right now she wanted nothing more than to have this woman's hands slip between her legs and show her all of the things she'd been missing.

"Let me take you upstairs," the stranger whispered, as if she'd read Marlena's mind.

Marlena froze for a millisecond, unsure of what her response should be.

*"Don't think. For once, just do!"* Vega's words from earlier rang in her head. *Just do.*

"Lead the way," Marlena replied, turning on her heel to face the woman for the first time.

She was devastating in a way that didn't seem fair. Her features were sharp, softened by the curly ash blonde hair falling around her face. Her eyes, the color of a sandstorm, drank in the sight of Marlena, setting her skin ablaze with need. Her legs went on for miles, drawing Marlena's attention. The woman wasn't much older than her but had the air of someone who had lived a thousand lives. Her confidence radiated off her in waves.

Marlena offered the woman her hand, and when she grabbed it, she could feel the heat under her skin.

*A fire-wielder.*

Without another word, Marlena followed her out of the crowd, where she was able to get a breath of fresh air sweeping through an open window.

She didn't catch sight of Arlet or Khort, but as she ascended the stairs, Marlena spied Vega in the center of the dance floor with a man she was sure neither of them knew. The man's lips met Vega's, devouring her in a heated kiss. The man didn't come up for air—it was like he was drowning and Vega was the only way he would survive. He treated her the way everyone always did, like she was the only person alive who mattered.

Marlena wanted to matter.

She wanted to be wanted.

And tonight, someone wanted *her*. Without the knowledge of who she was or what she could bring to their future. Or so she told herself. It wasn't often anyone mistook the Caelum sisters. Power made you known, and Marlena's succession of two seats wasn't a secret across the realm. That made it hard to go unnoticed.

If this beautiful stranger knew who Marlena was, she didn't let on, which made the spell she had on Marlena set deeper.

Her back hit a plush bed, and from there, the euphoria she felt when she settled into the party turned into something else—something more.

Marlena didn't know her name, and she didn't care, because when she moaned out, the woman between her legs murmured sweet words against her skin until her body trembled with pleasure.

"Good girl."

"Come for me again."

"Your body is fucking insane."

For the first time in her life, Marlena felt worshiped. Wanted.

*If only I could bottle up this feeling and save it forever.*

It was the longest trip back to Aeris ever.

The Caelums left a note that they would meet the girls back at home, so at least they'd have a few more hours to sober up before having to pretend like they hadn't gone to a rager in the heart of Amora last night.

Marlena, Vega, and Arlet watched the Feras take to the sky, soaring into the clouds until they were out of view, and then they loaded onto the boat that would take them back to the mainland, where they would then load into a transport vehicle back to Aeris.

At least the boat ride wasn't a long one.

The girls were feeling the repercussions of partying until the sun came up. Marlena's thighs were sore from her night with her midnight stranger, whose name Marlena never got—whose name she would never need—because the likelihood she would ever see her again was slim to none.

Arlet hung over the side of the boat, retching as they approached Fortis's docks.

"You better pull yourself together before we get home," Marlena warned, letting the cool air fill her lungs and clear her head of the lingering fog.

With little to no sleep, Vega and Arlet passed out as soon as their heads laid against the cushioned walls of their transport back to Stella.

Marlena, on the other hand, well, her reading was nowhere near done, and she was sure she'd hear about it later. She kept her nose in her book until they pulled into the gates of the estate. The white siding shone in the afternoon sunlight, reflecting into the vehicle and eliciting a groan from both Vega and Arlet when Marlena shook them awake.

"We're home. It's time to act normal." Marlena gathered her things, and when the door to the vehicle opened, there was a guard readying to unload their belongings.

"Miss Marlena, your parents are requesting your presence in the study," her father's chief guard said, motioning towards the path leading to the front door.

She looked back at her sister and Arlet, gave them a small smile, and told them she would see them for dinner. There was always something to do, somewhere to be.

Marlena was tired and had never wanted to shower more than she did right now... but that wasn't an option she was going to be given, and there was no sense in sulking about it.

She cleared her throat, nodded her head, and listened to the guard's footsteps as they made the trip into the house, up the grand staircase, and to the door of her parents' shared office space.

Marlena's knuckles rapped lightly on the door, and a small gust of her father's wind opened it. Their desks sat on opposite ends of the room, but in the center was a standing table where stools could be used for extra workspace.

Jonan and Ryanna stood in the middle, and as Marlena approached, she noticed pictures lining the entire length of the long rectangular table.

Her stomach dropped.

Evidence of last night's party was spread out along the table in this morning's *Tolevarre Chronicles*. It read: "Easy, Sleazy Caelum Sisters & Their Night Out in Amora."

Marlena felt her body go numb, and she forced herself to look up from the pictures to her parents.

"Would you care to explain what the fuck this is about?" Jonan asked through gritted teeth.

Most of the pictures were of Vega. Dancing with the guy Marlena had seen her with, making out with him, shooting back shots, and then finally... one of her sneaking off to the wine cellar where pictures were blurry—but it didn't take a genius to figure out what happened behind closed doors.

There were only a handful of Marlena, but there was no argument that they were her. In one of the pictures, Marlena seemed to be looking directly at the camera, and it caught her sneaking into that upstairs bedroom where Marlena had felt wanted for the first time in her life.

Ryanna tapped her foot, and for a moment, it was the only sound in the room while Marlena's eyes began to wander over the pictures laid in front of her again. "You can start speaking at any time, Marlena," her mother sneered.

Her eyes rose, catching her hateful stare. Marlena couldn't take this anymore. The hatred, the constant disappointment. She was at her breaking point... How much could one person take before they snapped?

"I'm curious..." Marlena started. "Am I supposed to have no fun in my life, ever?" Her head cocked to the side, watching her mother's jaw drop and her father's stupid fucking vein throb in his forehead.

He took a step forward, but Ryanna put her hand out, stopping him at the same time her jaw snapped shut. "You are to be the face of not only one, but *two* territories. You are to set an example at all times. Do you think this picture of you sneaking away with a lowly Ardor-born is setting an example of what the first ever double-seat-holding Curia member looks like?"

Marlena didn't think before speaking. "I think it shows I can do both. I can have fun and be the puppet you're plotting me to be." Because was she really being set up to rule on her own? No. It had always been her parents' plan to stay behind the scenes... to make

Marlena the face of two territories but never give her the control she wanted—the control she deserved.

The scoff from her mother came first. The raised palm that was projected to whack Marlena across the face came milliseconds later.

Except it never made contact.

Marlena caught it inches from her cheek. Maybe it was the hangover. Maybe it was that she was still drunk, but for the first time in her life, Marlena was done being used as her parents' personal punching bag.

She was done being abused.

Her grip around her mother's wrist was crushing, causing a pained gasp to slip from Ryanna's lips. Marlena didn't let go. She held her mother's hand in place, staring deep into her bright green eyes. "I've had enough. You're done. No more."

Ryanna tried to yank her hand back, but Marlena held strong, gripping tighter. "You're breaking my hand!" she whined.

"Good," Marlena responded. "This is what you've done to me my entire life. Caused me pain, crushed me, made me feel less than." Her father made a move to grab his wife, but Marlena used her wind to shove him back.

It caught Jonan off guard, and he stumbled, crashing into the table. The pictures of Marlena and Vega fluttered to the floor.

Marlena shoved her mother and used her invisibility to shuffle to the door without being seen. Before she snuck through, Marlena allowed herself to come back into view. She made sure her parents were looking at her when she spoke again. "You've had your fun using me as a personal stress reliever. Find someone else. It's time you treat me like the daughter you've raised... the daughter who can handle a little torture."

They could yell at her, scream, tell her she was a disappointment —it was nothing she hadn't heard before, but the physical abuse had run its course. This time, when Marlena left the room, she didn't hide herself behind her invisible cloak. She walked out, completely turning her back on her parents and the mess she'd made of their office.

*It's time to show them who they've raised.*

EIGHTEEN YEARS OLD

THE CLICKING OF MARLENA'S HEELS RANG DOWN THE LONG, guard-lined hallway.

Fortis had always made Marlena feel like there was someone watching her, and it was likely because there was. Lucius Dimico trusted no one, and neither did his father, or his father's father. There was a long line of untrusting commanders dating back to before anyone currently alive in Tolevarre could remember.

The Dimicos always had something to hide, and when there was always something to hide, there was always a shoulder to look over.

Marlena didn't hide, and she didn't look over her shoulder. She held her head high, making no eye contact with any of the guards as she walked by.

*Play the part.*

She was Marlena Caelum, future seat holder of Amora *and* Aeris. She didn't need a reason to show up unannounced to the fort city of Atrox, searching down the commander of Tolevarre.

She had only been to the commander's home once, but she knew where the meeting room was—and the meeting room was never far from the leader's personal office.

Two guards lined the double doors at the end of the hall, where Marlena knew she would find Commander Dimico. She took a deep breath and positioned herself in front of the doors, glancing idly at the guards in their fresh-pressed black uniforms.

They didn't even look at her, didn't pay her a single glance.

Marlena cleared her throat and crossed her arms like she'd seen her mother do a thousand times before when she wasn't getting the attention she desired.

The female guard's eyes landed on her, but not a muscle more moved besides her lips. "Commander Dimico isn't taking visitors."

Marlena motioned to the door. "Pity. He is now."

*Confidence, Marlena. Wear it like you own it. Make them bow.*

Finally, the male guard decided Marlena was enough of a nuisance to step in. "You'll have to come back." He started to move towards her, reaching for her arm—he would likely force her out of here if he deemed it necessary.

Marlena's invisibility washed over her. She stepped out of the guards' way, watching both their eyes blink rapidly as their faces flickered with confusion before she allowed herself to cloud back into view.

She was only a few feet away but far enough out of reach that she'd be able to disappear again if needed. "I'm only going to warn you once not to put your hands on me. If you do, I'll make sure to remove the air from your lungs."

She'd never tried, but she didn't mind using this man as a test dummy.

Marlena wasn't leaving this building without speaking to Lucius Dimico.

"Now, let's try this again." Marlena motioned to the door one more time. "Open the door for me. Or should I mention to the commander that his soldiers defy orders from the future Curia leader of Aeris and Amora? Please don't make me hold a grudge until it's my turn to rule."

The woman didn't hesitate this time, turning to grab her side of the double door. The man stared Marlena down, not budging an inch.

Marlena smiled slowly, letting it reach the corner of her eyes. "I'm an impeccable grudge holder." The soft smile her parents had taught her to have wasn't the one she donned now. The one taking its place was calculated, sinister. A promise.

Commander Dimico sat at his desk, focused on whatever paperwork was on it. His blond hair was slicked away from his smoky-blue eyes, and his cape hung over the back of his chair. The commander looked only a little ruffled from a long day's work.

"Marlena," he quipped as a half-assed hello. "Is there a reason you're here giving my guards a hard time and interrupting me unannounced?"

She stopped at the end of his desk, and the door to the office clicked shut from a small gust of her wind.

"Put a sound shield up." Marlena didn't ask.

Lucius's head snapped up, his pen falling from his fingers. "Excuse me?"

The commander obviously wasn't used to being bossed around, but that was okay... Marlena could work with that. "I'm sorry, I didn't realize I stuttered. Let me try again. Put a sound shield up." She didn't break eye contact. "Better?" A plan was beginning to form in her head, and a new sense of confidence had washed over her like a tide.

Lucius stood from his chair, and the grating sound from the legs scraping across the floor made Marlena twitch. She blinked away the fuzz inside her brain and crossed her arms over her chest lazily.

She waited, showing Lucius she wouldn't shy away from him. Marlena would no longer flinch when anyone approached her. *I am done being afraid. I've lived through worse.*

The sound shield fell into place as Lucius gripped the side of his desk, leaning forward to get within a few inches of Marlena. "Watch how you talk to me, little girl."

His warning should have frightened her, but it didn't—it settled something inside Marlena instead.

*He wouldn't be rattled if he thought I wasn't a threat.*

Her lip ticked up on the side. She enjoyed the reaction she'd gotten from Lucius. "I could give you the same warning, but I won't because I have something you want."

He laughed in her face, but only after he'd hesitated for a second too long. Just long enough for Marlena to catch it. Lucius pushed himself back, away from Marlena as he walked around to come face to face again without anything in his way. "Is that so?" His head cocked to the side, and Marlena saw the twinkle of amusement in his eye.

"Of course. You want power. It's why you sided with me on the day my parents tried to take mine away. Choosing my parents' side would take from you, wouldn't it?" Marlena was the one to cock her head now, imitating him. *Mocking him.* "They want to pretend there isn't a resistance, that the evil of this realm can be kept at bay if they give them just another crumb—throw them just one more bone, and they'll be happy."

Lucius was listening, the muscles in his body tightening as Marlena hit every nail on the head.

"They want the power to themselves. They think they're better than the rest of you, more powerful. That by having their daughter hold the seat to two Curia territories, they'll never fall. A well-placed puppet to keep their hands in the metaphorical cookie jar."

The commander's demeanor was calculated, etched from years of practice. His face gave away nothing, but Marlena could see the wheels turning behind his eyes... She could see his interest piquing by the way his sound shield grew stronger. His ability wrapped them in a tighter bubble to ensure they weren't heard by anyone else. "Is that what you are, Marlena? A well-placed puppet?"

*I was.*

Catching herself before she let self-pity slip through, Marlena waggled her head left to right, swallowing that nasty rising emotion down. "Not in the way they planned me to be."

Revenge was best served cold.

"I want to take it all away from them. Every last bit of power, of control they think they have. And if you follow along, I can give you everything you've ever craved, everything you deserve."

Promises. Her world had been forged off promises. The promise of a life no one else had. The promise of power.

And behind everyone's back, her parents would tell her how much she was allowed to have. They would only give her what they thought necessary while they basked in all they would keep from her.

Marlena was done being the puppet. It was time to become the master—to use what she'd been taught.

It was only a matter of time before the student became the teacher.

The hook was floating in the water, dangling by a bobber. All Lucius had to do was reach out and bite it. "And you plan on doing that how?"

Marlena adjusted Lucius's lapel. His eyes watched her delicate hands before shooting back to Marlena's siren-like gaze.

She could call him out to sea, but he would have to take the bait himself. "By taking them down from the inside. What better way to rid ourselves of both our problems at the same time than by doing so at the hands of the last person they'd expect?" Marlena raised her brow. That's exactly what her parents were—a problem.

A problem she only saw one ending for.

All her life, Marlena had been overlooked. By everyone, but mostly by her parents. They'd paid attention to Vega more—to the power that simmered beneath her little sister's skin. They didn't pay attention to the anger and hatred growing in their eldest daughter's heart.

She'd hid it well, and she would continue to hide it until the time was right. There was still much to do before Marlena made her strike. Her first order of business was to find the people who would fight behind her, people who were sick of being told what they could and could not do.

Lucius continued to study her. "And you think you're strong enough to do that?"

Marlena straightened her spine, standing up to her full height. She wasn't much shorter than the commander in her heels. "It's not always about physical strength," she mused. "I'm *smart* enough to do it... and at the end of the day, Commander, that's what it all boils down to. You have the brawn, congratulations, but I? I have the brain."

While everyone watched as Vega grew stronger, no one paid attention to how smart, how cunning Marlena was becoming or what she was studying when no one was looking.

She'd spent a lot of time being under the watchful eye while in public, assuring she didn't do or say anything she shouldn't... but no one watched when she was alone.

And when she was alone, Marlena had time to plot.

Her answer snagged him by his lip when he finally bit on the hook dangling out in the open. She already knew she had him hooked because she knew men like him. They just had to *think* they made decisions on their own.

"When are you making your move?" Lucius asked.

Taking a step back, Marlena began to roam around the room. She grazed her finger down the length of his desk, eyes landing on a map of Tolevarre so old she knew it was an original passed down through Fortis lineage. Lucius watched her every move.

"When the time is right." She pointed to the map. "When we have enough allies to do this once, and only once." People failed when they didn't take their time. Marlena wouldn't move too fast—

she would do this right. "This is a long game, Lucius. We're not overthrowing a multi-thousand-year-old government overnight. We aren't doing it in a week, a month, and certainly not a year." She leaned herself over the back of his chair, liking that the table had turned and she was on the other side. "We do this my way. Clearly, no one else your ancestors have put their trust in succeeded. Mira Viator, for example. She messed up, got caught, and your family pointed a finger at her like she was working alone. Like Fortis and Fraus haven't been in cahoots for hundreds of years trying to find new ways to crumble the very foundation our world was built on..."

His body froze at the mention of Mira. "Where did you get that information?"

Marlena's smile grew wider. "It's pretty easy to find what you're looking for when you know where to look." *And I've been looking for years.*

"If you're so willing to backstab the very people who birthed you, who's to say you won't do it to the people willing to side with you?" he asked, stalling.

A slight shrug of her shoulder was answer enough, but she would elaborate if it was the nudge Lucius needed. "I guess that's the risk you'll have to weigh out yourself, but let me remind you that my parents were willing to strip me of the only opportunity they'd ever given me. They've never cared about me. They didn't raise this daughter to love. They raised her to rule."

There was a break of silence where the two stared at each other in a battle of who would crack first.

*I'm done cracking.*

Lucius broke. "What all is in it for me?"

"What do you want?" Marlena cooed, pushing herself off the chair back, then meandering around to position herself in front of him again.

There was barely any hesitation in his answer. "I want control of

Fortis." Commanders didn't rule over their territories—they ran the army while another family member sat at the head of their seat. "I want a promise that my lineage, my son, will be the next commander of Tolevarre. He, as you were, was born to rule. Gifted by the gods to be stronger, better than anyone or anything before him."

Rumor had it Lucius Dimico's son, the one who had warned Marlena to stay away, was the strongest warrior their people had ever seen.

"That's all?" she asked.

"Marriage. You said you'd never be reduced to the birthing heir, but what if I can offer you a connection to Fortis and Fraus? Forever."

"I'm not interested in a three-way with you and your wife, I'm afraid," Marlena jeered. She knew where he was getting at, but the words had to be delivered outright. He had to make his demands clear.

He boomed a laugh, vibrating Marlena's insides. "While I won't deny your beauty, Marlena, I'm not interested in getting myself tied up with whatever madness you have going on inside that head of yours." He raised an eyebrow. "But my son, Bridger. A union with him would be a promise of power for years and years to come."

Marlena weighed her options. And the choice was easy. "You have yourself a deal." It wasn't a promise of love—love that Marlena had once craved. It was a promise of power, and power would get her farther than love. She stepped back, putting space back between them. "You're cordially invited to my parents' Saturnalia celebration. Bring your allies and your son."

Her heels matched the rhythm of her walk again as she strode for the door, her back to the commander. "If you don't show, I'll take that as your refusal to accept my offer, Lucius." The door opened on her gust of wind, the guards standing wide-eyed outside the door when it slammed open. "And I won't hesitate to do this without you.

I'll go to your allies next." Marlena glanced over her shoulder before she left. "And I doubt they'll want as much in return for a taste of the power I'm offering." She winked and strutted her way through the foyer, never looking back again.

*I am about to become my parents' worst nightmare, and it's exactly who they raised me to be.*

Mira Viator believed Fortis-born weren't fit to rule their territory but tried to summon the dead god who gave them their powers. Mars must have taken serious offense to that accusation, and if a god is offended, why would they answer back kindly?

IT WOULD NEVER MAKE SENSE TO MARLENA HOW SHE AND VEGA had such different beliefs. How had their parents managed to remind Marlena that their lineage was better than the rest, while simultaneously letting Vega form relationships with the help?

All of Tolevarre was born from the blood of the original gods, and some might argue they were all descendants, but it had been so long since then. The people who were from non-original bloodlines were so watered down now, Marlena believed they were hardly demigods at all. And others believed this too—her parents had reminded her to not act like a commoner all her life.

*They are less than us.* Her conversation with Vega replayed in her mind as a servant pinned her hair on top of her head.

Marlena's words were precisely the reason they weren't getting ready together for tonight's Saturnalia ball like they always did. Arguing with Vega hadn't been tonight's plan.

But when that fucking deer shifter—*what was her name? Delis?* —knocked Vega down, something inside Marlena made her want to—

"Miss Marlena, we have your dress ready," her personal maid commented from behind the doorway to her dressing room, interrupting Marlena's violent spiral of thoughts.

She nodded at the same time a knock on her door sounded, and

74

moments later her mother stepped through. "Oh, you're not dressed."

Marlena stood, taking a long, controlled breath through her nose and out her mouth. "I was just getting ready to step into the dress, Mother."

"Do you have an attitude already?" Ryanna asked, clasping her hands together after closing the bedroom door behind her.

She hadn't even had time to allow her servant to put the finishing touches on her makeup. The rosy blush was waiting on the table. "Of course not," Marlena pushed through gritted teeth.

Ryanna shooed the room attendants away with the flick of her wrist. It was the only dismissal either would get.

They scattered quickly, and Marlena didn't bid them goodbye—she didn't take her eyes off her mother, who floated on light feet to the table where the blush sat.

"Commander Dimico and his family are here." Ryanna slid her middle finger across the cream blush, stepping in front of Marlena. She gripped her chin, positioning her face before tapping the makeup onto the apples of Marlena's cheeks. Ryanna twisted Marlena's head from side to side until she was satisfied with the new color she'd brought to her daughter's face.

The words sent a chill down Marlena's spine, but she held her composure, waiting until her mother released her from her clutches. "Oh?"

*He's accepting my alliance.*

"The son," Ryanna started, disappearing into the dressing room to come out with the *prettiest pink* dress that made Marlena feel like she was ten again, "is interested in meeting you."

Marlena couldn't peel her eyes off the dress. "Mother, is it not time for a more age-appropriate look?"

Ryanna sighed. "Are you even listening to me?"

"How can I when that dress is so loud?" Marlena finally looked away from the garb, meeting her mother's stone gaze.

"It's a beautiful dress, Marlena." The pink was the color of the butchered pig they'd be feasting on at tonight's dinner. An assortment of different colored daisies rained down until they met in a pool of flowers around the bottom.

Marlena's eyebrow rose. "For a child, not the future leader of two territories." It was like her mother's goal was to ensure the people she would rule over and beside never took her seriously.

Actually, that was precisely what she was doing.

Ryanna huffed, throwing the dress to the floor. "I can never win with you. Have I ever done anything right in your life?"

Marlena wanted so badly to answer that question, but it was meant to bait her into an argument, and she wasn't in the mood. "I'm not wearing it. I'll find something else in my closet. Now let's talk about why you're really here." Marlena knew her mother hadn't come in here to help her get dressed—they had staff for that. "Bridger Dimico." She stepped over the poofy tulle on the floor, beelining for the dressing room, where a closet full of beautiful clothing waited for her.

Of course Ryanna followed. "So you do know his name."

Marlena fingered through her dresses. "Yes, Mother, I know the future commander of Tolevarre's name. I also know all the other future seat holders too. Should we go through a list and see if I get them right?" She came across a satin gold dress she'd worn underneath a fur-lined coat last winter. Her mother had said it was too revealing—*it's perfect.*

"You will watch your tone with me," Ryanna barked, taking a step forward.

Marlena spun around quickly, pointing a polished finger at her mother. "You will watch your next move."

Ryanna froze, her heels squeaking from the abrupt stop. "Or what?"

"Or I'll ruin the night and put an end to the very reason Lucius is here with his son. He wants a marriage between me and Bridger. He wants to unite the families."

Her mother's eyebrows drew together, but she corrected the movement quickly. *Never scowl. It causes wrinkles.*

As if they got wrinkles in the first 150 years of their life!

"Since when?" Ryanna asked.

Marlena dropped her dressing robe and stood completely nude in front of her mother. She unzipped the back of the gold dress and slid one leg in at a time. The satin gripped her hips tightly. Once she had the strapless top situated around her boobs, she turned her back to her mother. "Will you give me a zip?" Marlena made eye contact with her in the mirror, a memory of mirrors fluttering through her mind.

Ryanna's gaze scraped every inch of Marlena's body in her new skin-tight dress.

Ryanna scowled. "I asked you a question."

Marlena sighed, rolling her eyes and turning around while one arm held her dress in place. "Are you not the one who told me I needed to start building relationships with the other territory leaders?"

"Yes, but I figured that's what you've been doing in Littera." It was the first time either of her parents had brought up the time she'd been spending in Littera, and Marlena kept her lips sealed tight.

She didn't wait for her mother's help—she'd never get it. Marlena took a breath, concentrating on the way the air around her shifted through her open palm. With the flick of her pointer finger, Marlena sent a small burst of wind up her spine. Like the air had tiny fingers, it zipped the dress for her. Ryanna watched, hiding the wave of astonishment washing over her features as a sly smile slid over Marlena's pink painted lips. "If only you paid closer attention, I guess."

Marlena wiped the underside of her wrist across her lips,

smearing the pink lipstick. Gone was the sweet Marlena who played nice.

It was time to show people who she'd grown into. "Imagine what an alliance with Fortis would do. It comes with Ardor and Fraus. A ceasefire from all the trouble the territories have been causing. We could take control again."

*I can take control.*

Her parents' reign was coming to an end. Slowly but surely... it would fall.

And Marlena would be the one to take them down. They would beg for mercy, and if they were lucky, Marlena would let them live out their days in peace... locked away somewhere deep and dark where they couldn't hurt her anymore—where they could never touch her again.

"And you think you can pull this off?" her mother asked, watching Marlena as she slipped into a strappy pair of gold heels. "That you can get the Dimico boy to fall in love with you?" Ryanna followed Marlena into the main room.

Marlena leaned into her vanity mirror and traced a blood-red lip stain across her plump lips. She pressed them together, rolling her lips for the perfect application. Finally dressed and ready, Marlena turned around slowly. "I don't want love, Mother. I want power, respect. I want everything you've told me I don't deserve, and I want to watch you watch me get it."

Marlena didn't look back at Ryanna as she left the room on a gust of wind, pulling on the pin that held her hair up. Her straight blonde hair fell over her shoulders, settling down the middle of her back.

The party had already started, music from the live band pumping through the halls. Marlena kept her head high as she strode through the double doors, making her own entrance.

Heads turned, and the sound of whispers broke out amongst the guests in the ballroom. They were seeing the Marlena who was rising from the ashes, the girl who was no longer allowing herself to be treated as less than who she was—no longer standing in her parents' shadows.

The gold gown was a choice. A decision to pick the accent color of the wardrobe Marlena knew the commander and his family would be donning tonight—and every other night they were in the public eye.

A match made for revenge.

"Mar." Vega's voice broke through the chatter, her jaw agape with the slightest hint of a smile behind the shock. "Holy shit." She spun around Marlena, reaching out to touch the smooth satin of her dress. "You look amazing."

Their argument was still fresh in her mind. *It's like I don't even know who you are these days.* But Marlena pushed it aside.

This was her sister. Her Vega.

Marlena would save her. She would make sure Vega made it out alive, even if Marlena chose to burn the rest of the world down around them.

"It was about time I took charge of my wardrobe." Marlena had always been jealous of Vega's freedom, of all the choices she was allowed to make for herself that Marlena wasn't.

Vega's black ball gown was slit from the floor to her hip, with lace accents that gave peeps of her skin. The straps holding the dress up were thin, and her neckline plunged to above her navel. Vega's dark brown hair was pulled away from her face in her signature braids, but it fell over her shoulders in tamed waves. The smoky makeup accented the color of her eyes, and her lips were painted with nothing more than a pop of glossy burgundy.

Vega looked like a blooming storm on an autumn day. "I love it." She gave Marlena a small smile, and she could see the apology in Vega's eyes before she opened her mouth. "About earlier..."

Marlena held her hand up, ready to tell her it was okay, before they were interrupted by the sound of their father's voice. "Marlena."

Both daughters turned to face Jonan, whose attention was glued to the version of Marlena she'd chosen to present herself as. She didn't pay much attention to her father, because Commander Dimico loomed over his shoulder. His wife appeared beside him, and then his son.

Marlena hadn't seen Bridger since the meeting where his dad had determined her fate, and gods, had he grown. He was handsome then, with a jaw so sharp glass could be cut on it, but now? Now, he owned the body he lived in. Gone was a boy, and in his place was the confidence of a man who would one day command an army.

For only a second, their eyes met, and before Marlena could officially introduce herself, his gaze wandered... and when it did, Marlena watched his face soften, his eyes glazing over, and a muscle in his jaw ticked.

Marlena studied the man who should have been hers fall instantly head over heels in love with her little sister. It was clear as the morning sun rising behind the mountains of Stella.

The world could have spun a hundred times before anyone spoke, until Marlena realized anyone was speaking.

"Bridger, my daughter, future leader of Aeris and Amora. Marlena." Jonan gestured to Marlena, forcing Bridger's gaze off Vega.

"Marlena." He said her name like he was sucking on a sour candy. "Pleasure." Bridger grabbed her hand and placed a soft kiss on the back... but as soon as he was done, his eyes whipped back to Vega. "And your name is?"

"Vega," her sister answered with a gleam in her eyes.

"Vega." When he repeated her name, it was saccharine. He took his time. He greeted her in the same way he had Marlena, but with Vega, his lips lingered on her skin for noticeably longer, and the eye contact between them felt like everyone around them was interrupting a private moment.

"No wonder they've kept you away from us. A striking young man like yourself wouldn't last a night around a bunch of hormonal teens."

Marlena watched their back-and-forth banter. *Oh no.*

Vega was smitten... and when Vega caught someone's attention, it wasn't often she lost it. Khort, for example.

This was going to get ugly.

Lucius stared down his nose at Marlena, his eyebrows creasing in the middle—he realized it too.

*There's no going back, Marlena. You've made your decision. Now it's time to get what you've always wanted.*

## TWENTY YEARS OLD

DINNER ENDED, AND HER PARENTS DIDN'T LET HER GET VERY far before summoning her to a private meeting. Before she stepped through the doors to her parents' office space, she knew what the meeting would be about.

"Let's get this over with." Marlena strode in on a breeze of her own making. It wasn't often she opened a door with her hands anymore. Marlena was starting to use her powers to remind those around her of what she could do—she couldn't command the skies, but she could control the very air people breathed, and she could do so without being seen.

And sometimes that was scarier than the storms that came with warnings.

Ryanna sat atop her desk, legs crossed. Jonan stood on the other side, leaning lazily while eyeing Marlena as she walked in.

"It seems the deal you made with Lucius has gone up in smoke." Jonan stood to his full height, towering over her mother on the desk. Marlena got her height from him.

All of Stella heard the storm over Lake Mons, and everyone knew where it had come from. When Vega and Bridger didn't show up for dinner, the energy in the dining room grew tense. The two had been spending a lot of time together, but it was always with friends—*as friends*. Marlena spent her fair share of time with them, along with Khort and Arlet.

But it didn't take a scholar to see the two were hiding their feelings for the sake of others. The two weren't supposed to be together. Vega had been promised to Khort before she'd ever had the chance to choose for herself. Their parents had made that decision for her, for him—to better the chances of producing powerful offspring.

"You let your sister swoop in and take the one opportunity you might have had to hold some real power." Ryanna filed her nails aimlessly. Lately she made it seem as if anything to do with Marlena was a bore—like her eldest daughter wasn't even worth her attention.

It made Marlena want to crawl out of her skin—made her want to tear into her mother's just so she knew she was still there, to warn her of the problem she would become.

Marlena rolled her eyes. "Oh, please. As if holding two seats to the Curia isn't enough. I think I'll be just fine."

Jonan barked a laugh. "You think just because you've found a backbone means we're going to let you take control? As long as we're alive, Marlena, you will work for us. Under us. You've proven to us time and time again that you make childish decisions. We can sit at the head of our seats for as long as we'd like to make sure you don't destroy what we've worked for."

Marlena stared, blinking every so often. She schooled her face to masked calmness. "Do you plan on living forever?"

Her mother pushed herself off her desk, choking back an amused laugh. "Do you think this is a game?" She circled Marlena like a hawk, eyeing her up and down. "This isn't a game, Marlena. This is ruling. You can't fuck this up. You have to be willing to take what you want."

*Take what you want*, the voice inside her head mimicked.

"Are you saying I should have taken Bridger from my sister?"

Jonan sent a gust of wind to stop his wife from circling. Ryanna's hair fluttered to a stop around her *sweet, so pretty* face. She took a breath, closing her eyes until she exhaled. They jolted open, and a calmness washed over her. Jonan's air was a drug to her mother, a grounding agent when she got too wild. "I'm saying someone who is in the presence of power shouldn't allow it to be taken so easily."

Jonan wasn't innocent, but Ryanna... She was trained as a young woman to act this way by her own mother. It was the only way she knew.

Years of abuse trickled down to Marlena... and it would end with her. But she had to play her cards right. She'd already rebelled too much—she had to calculate her next move.

"They love each other. Isn't that what you want for her? To fall in love and be happy? To marry for the promise of a strong bloodline?" Marlena cocked her head, turning to face her mother. "Bridger's the strongest line you're going to get, I fear. And just because he doesn't want it with me, doesn't mean I'm useless."

"Yes, that is what we want. With Khort Fera. To keep the dragon line alive and strong," Jonan chimed in. They'd made a deal with the Feras a long time ago, and Marlena was sure it was more than just friendship the deal sealed.

Just because they were both strong didn't mean their children would get the dragon gene. "We all know that's not how that works."

Ryanna sneered. "Eventually it would. She could birth a few dragons and bring back our firing squad."

Everything was a strategic move for them. Maybe they didn't love Vega—they just needed to teach her *how to*.

Sighing, Ryanna walked back to her desk and took a seat when Jonan made his stance clear. "We will let her have her fun, but it won't last. Your job is to make sure the alliance with Fortis does. However you see fit."

*Oh, I'll make sure it sticks all right.*

Marlena would make sure, for her sake. Without another word, she turned and headed for the door. This was a game—a game of wits and who could outlast the other.

"If you need to spread your legs again like the night in Amora to get attention, then so be it." Her mother's voice followed her down the hall and clouded her mind well into the night.

Vega hadn't come home, and Marlena finished a bottle of wine before anyone walked through the garden. The patter of Arlet's light steps gave her away.

"Aren't you cold?" Arlet wrapped her arms around herself. She stood beside Marlena, who had been sitting on the stone garden wall for hours.

Marlena couldn't feel her butt anymore, but the alcohol helped with that. Over the last few years, she'd started to drink more, aching for the release it gave her. Marlena had never liked to be alone with her thoughts, and the older she got, the louder the static in her head became.

"I suppose I should be." Marlena hadn't been thinking about the cold.

Arlet's hair was pulled back in a ponytail, her tight curls bounding down her shoulders. She was in casual clothes, long since having changed from tonight's dinner attire.

She leaned forward against the chest-height wall, resting her elbows and propping her head up. "Wanna come inside? Your parents are gone." Arlet nodded behind her to the house. "Said they'd be back in the morning."

Marlena raised her brow. It wasn't often she didn't know where they were going. "Where did they say they were headed?"

Arlet shrugged. "I don't ask questions. I just figured you'd like to know so you can come inside and not risk freezing to death out here." She shivered, a gust of wind making her pull the collar of her coat higher.

Marlena grabbed hold of the wind with the feeling inside her chest and rotated it through the garden where they would be blocked from its new course.

Once Arlet pointed it out, the temperature continued to drop as the night wind started to pick up. The garden would start to hibernate soon. Most of the flowers were gone for the season, but the green foliage hadn't disappeared yet.

"I made muffins."

That got Marlena's attention. Arlet's mom's recipe was inimitable.

She slid off the garden wall, the heels of her shoes sinking into the moist ground. "And you're just now coming to tell me?" Marlena held up the end of her skirt, but it had already gotten a splatter of mud from when she'd come out here and trudged to the farthest corner she could find. "You should have led with that."

The warmth of the Aeris home wrapped around Marlena like a friendly hug. From the change in temperature, a chill shot up Marlena's and Arlet's backs at nearly the same time. The girls giggled, and Arlet's teeth began to chatter.

"I have a better idea!" She rubbed her hands together, yanked the plate of muffins off the counter, and hurried for the staircase.

Marlena followed, watching Arlet bound up the stairs.

"C'mon, slowpoke! A fire is calling our names."

Marlena heard the door to her room fly open and a little "oops" echo down the hall as she made it to the top of the stairs. She watched a muffin rolling towards her and bent as she walked, scooping it up to peek into her bedroom. A few more muffins lay scattered around the room.

"It's fine! I saved a few." Arlet smiled, holding up the plate at the same time another muffin hit the wooden floor. "Fuck."

Marlena laughed, and Arlet joined in. The girls fought off a fit of giggles as Marlena started picking the muffins up. It had been so long since Marlena laughed like that. "It's probably fine. The floors get cleaned almost every day, right?" She put them down on the coffee table in front of the hearth that was roaring with a fresh fire.

Arlet sat the plate down, careful not to lose any more muffins. "I had a fire lit before coming out to get you. Figured you'd be cold."

Growing up alongside Arlet had taught Marlena one thing: there was still goodness left in her darkening world.

Arlet was sunshine, through and through. Always thinking of others before her own well-being.

"Thanks…" Marlena didn't know what else to say—she wasn't used to being cared for. When she and Vega were kids, Vega would do caring, sisterly things for her, but over the last few years, so much had changed.

The sisters were changing, their lives splitting two separate ways.

Arlet waved her off, scurrying over to the fire to warm herself. She shuddered the closer she got to the heat rolling off the flames. "Oh my gods." She drew the words out slowly.

Marlena watched with a soft smile. She loved that Arlet was so carefree, never a worry in the world unless something completely detrimental happened.

*Must be nice.* Marlena cleared her throat and the thought from her mind. "I have an idea." She walked to her bed and pulled the big plush blankets and sheets to the floor, dragging them in front of the fire. Marlena yanked the pillows from her bed and the couches in the lounge off next, then fluffed them into a cozy pile on the floor. "Get comfy and warm up. I'm going to change."

Quickly, Marlena left the room and stripped into a satin pajama set with long sleeves and pants that hung off of her hips. It was her favorite sleep set, and it'd definitely seen better days, but she wasn't ready to part with it yet. She let her hair down, washed her face, and was back in record time.

The crackle of the fire was calling. She'd always loved getting lost in the flames.

Marlena dove into the plush covers, cuddling into the pillows for extra warmth. Once the girls were settled, they split a muffin down the middle. "Vega not coming home?" she asked Arlet, picking at her half.

Arlet's shoulders bobbed. "Not sure. I haven't talked to her since before she snuck off today."

Marlena eyed her. "She's okay, right?"

Chuckling, Arlet swallowed before nodding. "She's with Bridger. He'd rather drown himself in a puddle than let anything happen to her. She's more than okay." Taking her last bite, Arlet grabbed a deck of cards off the side table and dealt a hand to Marlena without asking if she wanted to play. "The real question is, are you okay?"

Arlet split the deck between the two without looking up. It was a mindless card game popular amongst kids, but it took a certain skill to win. Marlena usually wiped the competition out before anyone else had the chance. It was all about counting the cards and knowing where numbers went and in what order.

She watched Arlet's fingers graze over the cards delicately. "Of course I am... Why do you ask?" Marlena's eyebrows pinched together in question.

Arlet finished dealing the cards, wiping her hands together in habit. Khort used to accuse the girls of sneaking cards under their sleeves or hiding them under their wrists every single time they played—all because Vega cheated *once*, but only to mess with him. "You've just been a little reserved lately. I know you're busy, but sometimes I'm worried you're checking out on us."

Shadows from the fire danced across Arlet's face. Marlena watched them for a bit before replying. "There's always something to do. I would love a break, but alas, there is no time in my parents' schedule for that." Marlena took stock of the cards in her hand and started immediately crunching numbers. *What's missing?*

"But you're okay?" Arlet asked again as her hazel eyes wandered over the cards in her hand.

*No.* "Never been better."

Arlet rolled her eyes extra hard and set her cards down to focus on Marlena. "You know you can talk to me, right?"

Marlena drew a card, tossing it to the side to form a discard pile, and then looked at Arlet.

She must have had a look on her face because Arlet reached out and grabbed her free hand. "I know how it feels... to not feel good enough."

Nothing Marlena ever did would be good enough.

Arlet didn't talk much about her parents or how they'd left her behind—at least, not with Marlena.

Marlena wanted to squirm away from Arlet's touch, but she didn't. She forced herself to accept that someone would touch her because they wanted to comfort her, not because they wanted to hurt her.

Arlet pulled away, and the second her touch disappeared, Marlena felt the warmth spreading through her chest go with it. "We don't think that, by the way. That you're not good enough..."

*We.* As in her friends—Vega, Bridger, Khort.

"Sometimes they make me believe it," Marlena admitted before she could stop herself.

Marlena watched Arlet's face fall. "It's hard to be the eldest child, huh? It comes with responsibilities we didn't ask for."

Arlet was supposed to run Vates—before it fell. She was the oldest, but her brother and sister got the power. Her parents never gave up hope that Arlet would one day come across her own.

But sitting here, across from Vher, Marlena found herself wondering if Arlet's power just wasn't one that could be seen. Because she could make you believe everything was all right. She'd always been like that. Arlet had been born to rule, too, but her blood hadn't gotten the memo...

Arlet played her next move while Marlena watched what she laid down.

Marlena shuffled the cards around in her hand, knowing she was able to end the game with what she currently held... but she didn't want to. "I want the responsibility. I know I can handle it. I just wish someone would believe in me."

Arlet laid her cards down, beating Marlena at her own game in nearly one hand. "I believe in you."

The smile overtaking Marlena came for two reasons. One, because it felt nice to hear someone say they believed in her, and two, because Arlet *would have* kicked her ass almost instantly—if it weren't for the last hand she hadn't thrown down on purpose. "Someone's been paying attention."

"I've watched you beat everyone hundreds of times. It's given me a lot of time to analyze the moves you make. Let me see your hand." Arlet leaned forward, trying to get a glance at the cards Marlena had fanned out.

She pulled them against her chest and shook her head, leaning away from Arlet, who slinked in closer. "Nope."

"Oh, come on," Arlet whined, continuing to invade Marlena's space. She shifted to her hands and knees, crawling the few feet separating them. "You're being shady! Did you let me win?"

Marlena laughed, leaning until her back was nearly flush with the floor. Holding the cards above her head, she did her best to keep them away from Arlet. "Nooooo, I would never *let* someone win."

Arlet's grabby hands didn't stop.

Marlena had to uncross her legs quickly, trying to wiggle away from Arlet's pursuit. "Then show me them!" Arlet giggled, crawling into Marlena's lap.

"Never!" Marlena pushed Arlet's hands away with her free hand, sliding the one with the cards behind her back.

Arlet straddled her, attempting to reach around Marlena to rip the cards from her. Marlena shuffled them between two hands before pushing her power into the cards to shield them from sight. They were still there, and Arlet would be able to find them if she reached out and touched them. Marlena pulled her hands up in front of her, threading the cards through her fingers, and to Arlet, it would look as if nothing were there.

A sneaky smile pulled at Marlena's lips. "If you guess which hand they're in, I'll let you see them."

Arlet leaned back, resting her butt on her calves. She still stayed on Marlena's lap... and Marlena couldn't help but think about how she liked the weight of Arlet on top of her. The smell of her honey shampoo was unmistakable with her this close.

Arlet nibbled on her lip as she considered which hand to choose. Marlena's eyes flicked away when she realized she was staring.

"Fifty-fifty shot here, Arlie. What's it gonna be?" It had been so long since Marlena used her nickname.

*"Using nicknames makes you sound lazy."* Why did her mother's voice have to pop in at some of the worst times?

*Get out of my fucking head,* Marlena said to the lingering voice echoing in her skull.

Arlet's eyes settled on Marlena's right hand, and by the look in her eyes, Marlena knew she knew where the cards were before she even nodded in their direction. Arlet made a move to reach for them, but before she could make contact, Marlena shoved them down her top, securing them against her ribcage. Pulling her hand out of her satin shirt, she opened both palms wide, showing Arlet the cards were gone. "I guess you were right." Marlena made quick work of trying to get out from underneath Arlet, but she wasn't quick enough. Arlet reached inside her shirt to fish them out.

Marlena stashed them there knowing Arlet wouldn't follow them down... *Gods, was I wrong.*

Arlet's hand grazed over the peak of her breast, her nipple pebbling from the friction. Marlena bit her lip to hide her gasp.

Arlet groaned in defeat, eyes lapping up her loss with the cards now in her hands. She over-pouted, sticking her bottom lip out. "You would've beat me."

Marlena swallowed, trying to find her words. *Arlet is on top of me, and I like the way it feels... I like the way it felt when she slipped her hand down my shirt.* Marlena opened her mouth to speak, and finally Arlet crawled off. With the extra weight gone, Marlena inhaled sharply, finally getting the air she needed to clear her head.

*She's your sister's best friend, you fucking idiot.*

Arlet cocked her head and raised a brow, waiting for a response.

*She's your friend. Your friend.*

"I didn't think you'd stick your hand down my top." Those were the words Marlena decided to go with once she could speak again. Smooth.

Arlet shrugged, laying Marlena's cards on top of the pile. "They're just boobs. You think I'm scared of a nice pair of tits?" She shook her head.

Did Arlet *like* women? Marlena had no idea. Arlet had never been as open about what she did in her sex life as Vega was.

"Nice pair of tits?" Marlena asked, feeling flushed. All thoughts of the stupid cards gone.

"Yeah, they're definitely your best asset. Among other things like your brain, but if you ever wanna get anyone's attention, just hike those babies up and wear something low-cut. You'll get your point across quickly." Arlet mixed the cards up. "Wanna go again? And this time can you not let me win?"

Marlena laughed, brushing off the buzz in her body as drinking too much wine and being warm by the fire. "Sure, but you better play like you want it. I won't let you win twice," she said with a wink.

Arlet waggled her brows and settled back into her spot.

The game was over in under five minutes. Marlena won, and Arlet sighed, followed by a yawn. "I guess we need a rematch, but please, another day. I'm so tired," Arlet whined.

Marlena felt the drowsiness of the day taking over during the last game. "Me too."

Arlet went to stand, but Marlena reached out to put her hand on her thigh, stopping her. "Will you stay?" she whispered, her voice almost drowned out by the crackling fire. "I don't want to be alone."

*I'm always alone.*

Pausing, Arlet looked down at Marlena's hand, and then slowly, she nodded once. "Yeah. Yeah, I can stay."

A tired smile crept onto Marlena's face. "We can move to the bed."

"No, I like it here. Brings back memories." Memories of their childhood when they'd do this downstairs in front of the main fireplace during sleepovers.

Arlet moved pillows around while Marlena knocked the logs in the fire off one another with a poker to spread the embers and kill the roaring flame to a simmer.

Marlena settled beside Arlet, who was facing her way on a nearby pillow. She smiled sleepily as Marlena slipped under the warm blankets.

The second Marlena started to feel warm and sated, Arlet slid her frozen toes between her closed thighs, leeching the warmth from between them. The intrusion made Marlena twitch and grit her teeth.

Arlet laughed sleepily. "Sorry, very cold. Need to let them thaw." She'd always done this—her toes were like icicles.

But this time, with her so close and her legs wrapping up with Marlena's, it felt *different.*

Marlena watched as Arlet drifted into sleep, her lips slightly parted and breathing through her mouth with long, slow inhales.

Before the fire lulled her to sleep, Marlena remembered the warning echoing through her mind...

*Don't let her get in the way.*

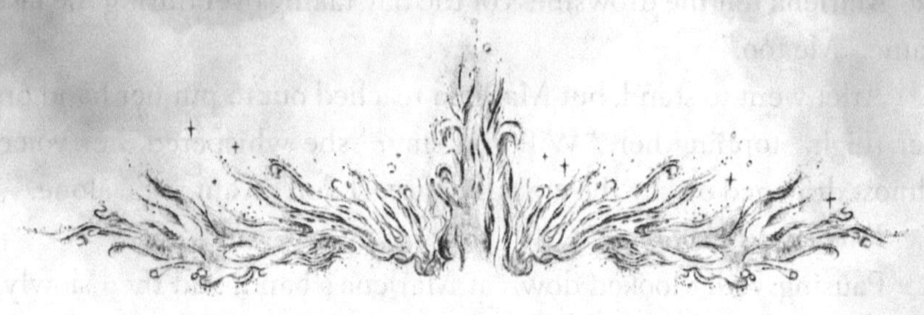

## Twenty-One Years Old

MARLENA LEANED OVER THE DESK WITH HER ARMS LOCKED AT the elbows, staring Lucius down. "What are you saying, Lucius?" She wouldn't give him the satisfaction of calling him by his title... not when the Ignises were sitting at the other end of the desk, their attention focused on her.

"I'm saying... that Bridger will get bored of her, like he did with all the other girls before. Bide your time; he'll come around. Even if I have to make him."

Zetta, the Curia member of Ardor, and her husband, Miklov, who was also a master of fire wielding, tried to hide their shock at his words. They were allies, ready to fight when everything finally blew up in their faces, but it was clear their strong suit wasn't what came before the fight... They wouldn't be the brains of this operation.

And as much as Lucius wanted it to be him who called the shots, everyone in this room knew who had the upper hand.

Marlena would make sure to remind them every chance she got.

A cackle bubbled from Marlena's chest. "Do you think I can't do this without an arranged marriage with your son? That was merely a requirement on your end—something *you* wanted. I couldn't care less about who your son is or isn't fucking. He's handsome, but I don't beg."

Lucius let an eerie smile slide over his lips. "Is that how you think you'll convince your sister to join you when this all comes to a head? Tell her you let her keep her man and hope for the best?"

Marlena leveled a glare at him. "Why don't you let me worry about my sister, hm?" She cocked her head to the side. "You focus on your army, on getting them ready."

Miklov finally spoke, spearing through the tension rising between Marlena and Lucius. "What's your plan, Marlena? You keep talking about overthrowing your parents, but you make no moves, and you keep quiet about what your *actual* plan is, almost as if you don't have one. We've been biding our time for years."

Her head snapped to Miklov, her lip tilted upward in a sneer. "The more people who know what I'm planning behind closed doors, the bigger the chance of us getting caught and beheaded before we can actually do anything at all." Marlena removed her hands from the desk, standing straight. "There are two choices here." She held up two fingers, wiggling them for emphasis. "You trust me and follow behind, knowing I'll make it worth our while in the end. Or you don't." There was a dainty pop of her shoulders before she grabbed her coat from the back of a chair. "The way I see it, you're either with me, or you're against me."

Marlena slid her arms into the fur-lined coat and fit it over her shoulders. "I've said this before and I'll say it again. I will do this with or without you all. Choose your side." She strode for the door. "And you'd better do it quickly, because I won't wait. When the time comes, I'll strike."

The door of Lucius's office opened on her wind, and Marlena strutted out, leaving them to talk about her behind her back.

Marlena wasn't afraid. She would do this without allies if she had to—but she knew, *knew* that Commander Dimico and the Ignises would fall in line. They'd been waiting for this chance for hundreds of years, trying to seep into the minds of their people and get them to do the dirty work... and now, finally, someone was giving them the opportunity to follow along without having to be the ones to figure it out logistically.

All they had to do was ready their people and fall in line when the time came.

Marlena descended the stairs into the main house, and people dared to watch as she rounded through the Dimicos' home like she owned the place. Her confidence was growing. Finally, she was crawling out of the shadows her parents had trapped her in.

People moved out of her way, the heels of her pointed boots the only warning anyone got that she was behind them.

The guards standing outside the home's training room didn't falter like they had the first time Marlena had shown up here. They opened the doors as soon as she approached.

Khort sat on the side of the large training ring, sweat dripping down the bridge of his nose. Arlet sat beside him, a dagger sliding through her fingers like it belonged there. Her attention flicked from the ring where Vega had Bridger pinned on his back with a knife to his throat, to Marlena barging in like she owned the place.

Arlet relaxed into a smile, and the simmering anger from Marlena's meeting upstairs seemed to melt away. She swallowed, smirking at her before forcing herself to look away. "Damn, you're really going to let her beat you like that?" Marlena leaned against the ring, focusing on Bridger.

He answered with a laugh, twisting his body in one swift move to flip their position. Bridger pinned Vega's hand over her head, knocking the blade free. He tossed it to the edge of the ring, out of Vega's reach. "I gotta let her think she has the upper hand every once in a while." He winked, leaning forward to press a quick kiss to Vega's lips before he hopped off, extending his hand to help her off the mat.

"Your turn?" he asked Marlena, nodding to Khort. "He's looking for a rematch since I kicked his ass three times in a row."

Khort grumbled, fleeing his seat to get a drink of water.

They'd been spending a lot of time here in Fortis, learning the ways of the warriors. It had been Marlena's idea, reminding her sister and friends that being experts of battle was important. With the uprisings in Ardor and Fraus, they all needed to learn to protect themselves better. Marlena and Vega had a little training growing up, but not enough. They didn't know it now, but war would come... and Marlena wanted them to be ready.

That voice in the back of her head began to stir. *Vega will never follow you.* Marlena felt like she had to physically remove those thoughts from her mind—like nails on a chalkboard, she clawed until she could no longer hear the doubt creeping in... but the echoing of the voice that wasn't hers was still there.

The uprisings in Ardor and Fraus were similar to the one that took Vates down, but there was one big difference.

The people who were winding up dead now were the ones who supported the current leadership, not seers.

Vega looked Marlena over, her stare slicing through. Sometimes she swore Vega could see inside her brain. Before Vega could ask what Marlena knew was coming—*what's wrong?*—she shook her head to clear her thoughts and responded to Bridger's question.

"As fun as it sounds to piss him off some more, I have a few things I need to get done back in Aeris tonight. I'm heading out. Just wanted to see if you were coming with me?" Marlena gritted her teeth, focusing on the right here, the right now and not the echo of a voice she couldn't seem to control.

Vega shook her head. "I think I'll stay with Bridger."

Arlet stood. "I'll go back with you so you don't have to ride alone."

Marlena searched her hazel eyes for a hint of what she was thinking. "Great." Arlet and Marlena were spending more nights where it was just the two of them lately. Now that Vega and Bridger weren't sneaking around, pretending not to love one another, they were attached at the hip, leaving Arlet with plenty of free time.

Not purposely, but Arlet was definitely giving them their space, and it was clear there was no ill will harbored either.

Truly, the two were disgustingly obsessed with each other. Marlena couldn't blame Arlet for backing off. She couldn't understand the appeal of a love like theirs. It seemed rather exhausting, really.

Arlet hugged Vega and Bridger and waited to say goodbye to Khort, who decided to leave with them.

He hated watching Vega fall in love with someone else. Khort wouldn't admit it, but everyone knew—everyone could see the way he'd avert his gaze whenever they kissed, or how he'd started to use whatever excuse he could to leave instead of staying the night like he used to.

Marlena didn't hug anyone goodbye. She rarely let anyone touch her anymore. Since her parents had stopped physically beating her, Marlena didn't crave touch like she once had. When the only time anyone touched her was when they were hurting her, Marlena craved anything but that. She wanted someone to caress her cheek, to hold her and not let the world hurt her anymore.

But now, the idea of someone's hands on her brought back the memories she was scared of seeing, of the vulnerability she'd been working too hard to diminish.

After Arlet hugged Khort, Marlena stepped back, putting distance in between them. "Get home safe." That was the only goodbye he would get. She turned on her heel, and the driver opened the door to the large transport vehicle.

Marlena settled herself in the seat facing the way they were driving, watching as Arlet slipped and claimed the bench across from her. The door shut with a click, and the engine roared to life.

For a while, they rode in silence, Arlet fighting off sleep and Marlena lost in a book she'd gotten years ago from Littera.

Arlet stretched her arms over her head and wiggled her hips against the seat like she was a cat looking for the comfiest spot to nap.

"Wake me up when we get there." She smiled sleepily. "Bridger wore me out. I don't know how Vega keeps going." Marlena watched her weigh it out in her head. "Well, I do, because Vega can't ever sit still... but gods, I'm sore," she whined.

Marlena paused in the middle of reading a sentence. "Want me to rub your back?" she asked, shocked by her own question.

She'd just been internally freaking out about the idea of someone hugging her, and now here she was, offering to rub Arlet's overworked muscles.

Arlet's features warmed, a delicate tinge of pink working its way into her cheeks. She didn't say anything, only nodded.

The vehicle picked up speed on the back roads leading through the outskirts of Fortis. Marlena closed her book and hid it between the cushions.

Arlet clipped her hair up, exposing her neck and the sweater draping over her shoulders. Spring was in full bloom, and the chill had yet to leave the air as the sun began its descent through the sky.

Marlena pulled her leg up underneath her, making room for Arlet to sit in front of her on the bench seat. She cracked her fingers, trying to loosen her hands while untangling the webs around her brain. *This is just Arlet. You've touched Arlet before. Arlet is your friend. This isn't weird. Touching Arlet isn't weird.*

She lowered her hands to Arlet's shoulders, her touch featherlight until she felt Arlet settle in closer. Marlena's thumbs dug into the muscles surrounding her spine at the base of her neck.

Training with Bridger was hard—he didn't back down, and it was clear he wasn't willing to change his fighting style to go easy on any of them either.

Marlena appreciated that.

She squeezed Arlet's shoulders, really digging into a knot around her scapula. She inhaled hard, and Marlena naturally softened her touch.

Arlet twisted her neck from side to side. "No, no, that felt good."

Her voice was hazed with satisfaction, and Marlena was sure if she could see her face, her eyes would have rolled back into her head.

Marlena drilled her thumb into the spot again, her other hand wandering to the same muscle on the opposite side, pressing in with the bottom of her palm.

Arlet leaned in for more, chasing the hard press of Marlena's touch. "Fuuuuuuck," she groaned, and Marlena inhaled her scent as Arlet's neck came within inches of her nose and lips.

Honey mixed with the smell of Arlet's dried sweat. It should repulse her, make her crawl out of her skin at the thought of touching someone who had yet to shower after a lesson in the ring... but it didn't.

Marlena wanted more. She licked her lips and allowed her hands to slide up to the edges of Arlet's loose sweater. She slipped her fingers underneath and pulled it off her shoulders. It sank between them, catching in the crook of Arlet's elbow, revealing more of her soft skin. Arlet didn't protest. The opposite, actually. She pulled her arms out, leaving her in a sheer tank top.

The heat of Arlet's skin made the outside world fall away. It was just Marlena and Arlet, trapped in their own universe.

Marlena drove her fingers back into Arlet's achy muscles, and this time, a moan slipped through Arlet's lips. Marlena couldn't help it—she'd lost all her senses but one. She leaned in, her lips fluttering over the delicate skin of her neck. Goosebumps scattered over Arlet's skin, and she gasped. "Mar..."

The nickname was a whisper, but it made something inside Marlena click. The way Arlet drove into her touch, her eagerness to accept the massage—all of it had Marlena's head spinning.

Arlet wanted this too. It wasn't just a figment of Marlena's imagination.

Marlena slid a hand up and cupped Arlet's throat where it met her chest, driving her fingers into her collarbone.

Arlet's chest rose, her lips parting. Taking Marlena by surprise, Arlet shifted her hands from her lap, and one reached behind to grab Marlena's exposed thigh. The other slid up Marlena's arm until it rested against her wrist. Gripping her softly, Arlet guided her hand up higher on her throat, stopping when the new position was underneath her jaw.

Marlena tightened her grip only a little but yanked Arlet's body against hers, her ass arching in between Marlena's thighs.

The gasp Arlet let out ruptured any control Marlena felt she had. Her lips met Arlet's exposed neck, kissing up the side and then sliding her tongue all the way down to her collarbone.

"Gods, Marlena." Arlet let out a sigh, her hand wandering up Marlena's thigh, higher and higher.

The vehicle shuddered, and without another warning, the sound of the engine seizing and grinding against itself pierced through the cabin. Both girls' hands shot up to cover their ears at the same time the vehicle lurched to a violent stop.

Arlet went flying to the floor at the sudden halt, and Marlena barely caught herself against the cushion on the other side.

Rattled, Marlena reached for the door, noticing a billow of smoke rising from underneath. Her head spun, and the lust clouding her senses evaporated. "Get out," she stammered. "Arlet, get out." She pulled Arlet by her arms. She had already begun to pick herself up—but she wasn't moving fast enough.

Marlena pushed Arlet through the door's opening before following, landing roughly in the mud. It had started to rain, a light but steady drizzle causing the overheated transport to steam.

She would probably be steaming too if that were possible... her body still trying to come down from the high of Arlet's need.

*She wanted me.*

They made eye contact as the driver trampled through the mud to get to them. "Are you girls okay?" He looked them over, scanning their bodies for any visible injuries.

"I think I'm okay, yeah." Arlet spoke first, nodding her head at the obvious question Marlena was waiting to have answered too.

"What the fuck was that?" Marlena tried to keep her voice relaxed, but it came out strained, a taut rope pulling at every muscle in her body.

"The engine locked up. I'm not sure. It happened so quickly," he stuttered.

Marlena moved around the front, pointing to the hood. "Well, open it."

He did, and more steam rose from the open hood. "I'm going to have to call for a replacement vehicle. You two should get back inside and get out of the rain."

Marlena shook her head violently. "I don't trust anything with an engine that smokes. What would happen if that thing blew up and you lost not one, not two, but *three* future Curia seats because of your incompetence?"

The man grew paler. "You're right, I—I'm sorry, Miss Marlena."

"You need to—"

"Marlena." Arlet's soft voice mirrored the gentle touch of her hand resting on her forearm. "It's okay. He'll get it figured out." Droplets of water slid down Arlet's exposed arms, and the cool spring air made her shiver. "There was an inn with a tavern underneath a few miles back. We can go hang out there while he handles it."

A loud rickety cart led by a couple mules rolled towards them. Their guard's eyes followed Marlena's, and he visibly let out a sigh of relief, rushing into the road with his arms flailing.

The woman driving the cart pulled up beside him, but he was too far away to be heard.

"Don't be rude to him. He didn't do anything." Arlet's hand stayed on Marlena's arm for another few seconds, pulling her attention away from their guard. "He's doing what he can to help."

Marlena was unable to get the image of Arlet's body pressed up against hers out of her mind. "Yeah, well, I need to get home, and now we're stranded," she huffed.

Arlet chuckled, reaching inside the cab for her sweater. She slipped it on, hiding herself from the cold rain coming down. "And for now, there's nothing we can do." Arlet pulled Marlena's bag out and tossed it to her. "So, we might as well make the best of it."

As if all of the heat she'd felt had vanished, Arlet headed towards the guard and the covered cart. She peeked over her shoulder, a cheeky smile pulling at her lips. "Are you coming or are you gonna just stand in the rain and mud?"

Marlena watched her hips sway and blinked a few times before snapping out of her trance. Like a striking snake, Marlena pulled the book from between the cushions of the vehicle and stuffed it in her bag before the rain ruined it, trailing after Arlet.

"I'm on my way to Fortis, so I can give him a ride back and drop you ladies off at the tav to stay warm. It'll be a few hours before he's back though. My mules don't go quite as fast as that fancy thing." The woman pointed at the still steaming military vehicle, her voice deep and weathered. She gestured to the back. "You ladies ride back there where it's warm."

Marlena helped Arlet up and held on to her hand as she hoisted herself into the wagon behind her. The ride was bumpy, and the wheels rattled too loudly to have a real conversation. So they sat in silence... and it didn't feel awkward.

Before long, they were climbing back out of the wagon and running through the rain that had begun to fall angrier than before. Where was Vega when they needed her?

Thunder roared in the distance, lightning sputtering across the sky. Marlena jumped, seeking shelter under the awning of the tavern's entrance.

Arlet laughed, wiping her face with her soaked sweater. "Hopefully they have a fire we can dry out by." She opened the door for Marlena, and they both slipped inside together.

Inside the tavern, music was played by a man with a small guitar. The melody of the song felt upbeat, but the lyrics were dark and alluring. People danced, drank, and cuddled into tight corners, but somehow, there were a couple open seats near the fire.

They hurried over to them and slipped out of their jackets. Marlena's fur coat got some looks, but when didn't she draw attention? The faces around here knew her.

Everyone in Tolevarre recognized Marlena.

She was plastered all over news bulletins and during important broadcasts every week.

Once the next Curia seat holder got to a certain age, the people of Tolevarre began to notice, starting to watch what kind of ruler they would be faced with in the future.

Rumors were swirling about Marlena—she was known as snappy, quick-witted, and unforgiving.

They weren't wrong.

She ignored the looks, happy to feel the top of her dress had been saved from the rain. Arlet, on the other hand, was soaked through. She got as close as she could to the fire without burning herself or falling in after hanging her saturated sweater.

A barmaid came by and handed them both a large mug of ale.

"Thanks, Sunny!" Arlet said with a bright smile on her face as if they were old friends.

Marlena was bad at remembering all the faces she'd come into contact with. All except for the ones that mattered. Marlena sat in the chair closest to the fire and took a sip of the wheat-flavored ale.

Her insides started to warm after taking a couple more big swigs. Marlena shivered once as a jolt of cold shot down her spine. "I am so sick of the cold," she groaned.

Arlet gulped the ale in her mug quickly, aiming to do the same thing Marlena was—get warm. "We should go dance. That'll warm us up."

Marlena eyed her and then let her gaze sweep over the crowd, who'd finally gone back to paying attention to whatever it was they'd been fixed on before the two walked in.

Arlet always wanted to dance, and she'd always been good at it. So while she didn't have a "power," per se, she was powerful in other ways. She could dance, carry a tune better than anyone Marlena personally knew, and grab any attention she wanted by merely existing.

Arlet was unlike anyone Marlena had ever met.

And tonight, she'd made it clear she wanted her too... Marlena wasn't alone in these newfound feelings.

"Okay. Let's dance." How could she say no? They were known to be friends. If anything got back to the people closest to them about a wild night after breaking down on the outskirts of Aeris, no one would suspect anything nefarious.

*We're just friends.*

It is said that the gods will only take what you're willing to give them, but just because they take, doesn't mean they give in return.

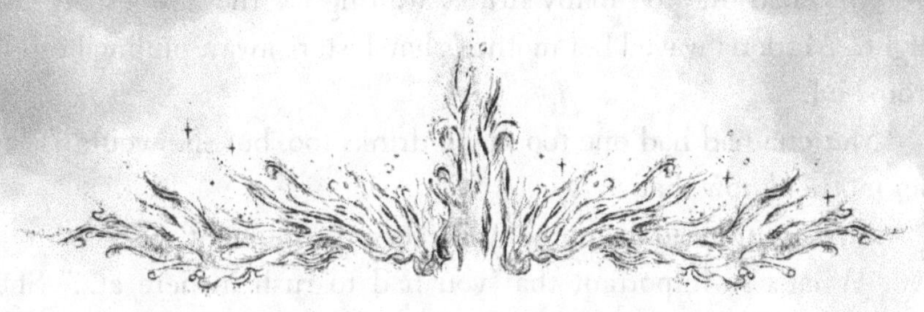

## Twenty-One Years Old

"Good morning." Ryanna barged through Marlena's door unannounced. "Get dressed. Your father and I need to talk to you."

Marlena peeled one eye open, fighting the urge to yank the covers over her head. She didn't groan because she didn't have the energy to argue with her mother about it if she did.

*"Groaning makes you sound uncivilized."*

She and Arlet hadn't gotten home until the early morning hours after their vehicle had broken down. By the time the guard came back with a replacement ride, the girls were wasted off the inn's cheap ale.

They were both curled up in Marlena's bed, cozy and warm, when Ryanna's gaze finally landed on Arlet, who could sleep through anything, sleeping soundlessly beside Marlena.

Marlena sat up, tracking her mother's gaze. It wasn't unlike the girls to have sleepovers, but it had been years since they'd had a real one... Or at least, that was what everyone thought. Marlena and Arlet had begun to have them again.

Regularly.

And last night, nothing else happened. Their moment in the cab of the military van had come and gone—but the feel of her lips hovering over Arlet's pulse still lingered.

"She had one too many drinks waiting for the new escort last night." Marlena waved her mother's harsh stare away, pulling herself from bed.

Marlena had had one too many drinks too, but she wouldn't let her mother know that.

That would lead to another unnecessary argument.

"What's so important that you had to rush in here at..." She paused, looking at the ticking clock on her wall. "Six in the morning?" Marlena rubbed her eyes, trying to wake herself from a sleepless daze.

"Get dressed and get to the meeting room." Ryanna stormed out, slamming the door hard enough to rattle the walls and decor hanging on them. A mirror wiggled off a nail and crashed to the floor. Somehow it didn't break.

Marlena could only imagine what was waiting for her in the meeting room if her mother was *this agitated* so early in the morning.

Arlet stirred, groaning at the light coming through the open curtains. "Five more minutes."

Arlet and Vega were so similar sometimes.

Marlena smirked, rolling her eyes as she slipped out of her sleeping gown and into a quick outfit. She opted for a flowy emerald dress, with a black belt that cinched her waist and gave her chest a lift. "I have to meet with my parents," she told Arlet, running a hand down her exposed arm. "Sleep. I'll find you later."

Marlena quickly tied a pair of black thigh-high boots up her legs, brushed her teeth, and pulled her hair into a tight ponytail before quietly leaving the room. Once she shut the door, her demeanor changed. She didn't walk on quiet footsteps. She owned the space she took up.

Her parents were waiting for her when the doors to their study opened, but they weren't alone.

Ryanna's younger sister was sitting next to her, and beside Marlena's aunt was her cousin. Ivelle Fugere.

Her chartreuse eyes, which were almost the exact same color as her mother's, met Marlena's, and she held her stare, glaring like she'd been forced against her will to be here.

Ivelle was a few years older than Marlena, and despite being family, she didn't come around much—from what she understood, Ivelle was known to be a bit of a problem child. Marlena would bet money that her bad attitude was linked to the fact she was missing out on a Curia seat. If it weren't for Marlena and her double abilities, Ivelle would have been next in line for Amora.

Though, somehow, Marlena was sure her parents would have manipulated a way to sneak Vega in over Ivelle.

*It was never meant to be hers.*

"Marlena." Celeste Fugere smiled, lighting up the room. "Long time no see. You're as beautiful as ever." Her red hair matched her daughter's, but the smile on her face was polar opposite of the scowl on Ivelle's.

Marlena cocked her head to the side, ignoring Celeste's kind words, and focused on her parents. "What's this about?"

"Have a seat, Marlena," Jonan ordered. Marlena had fallen asleep on cloud nine, wrapped up in the sheets with Arlet... hoping for a much different scenario upon waking up.

Now, Marlena stood rigidly across the table from her family. "I think I'll stand."

Her mother rolled her eyes, huffing through her nose. "Must you two girls always be so difficult?"

Ivelle gawked at Marlena's brazen lack of fear of her parents. Marlena raised a brow, as if she were saying, *What are you looking at?*

Ivelle snapped back to the grumpy child she was portraying herself as, looking away first, while Marlena stayed the ice-cold future leader.

Jonan spoke with his booming voice. "Marlena, we have a

proposition for you. One we think you'll really, really like... if you're up for a challenge."

*I'm always up for a challenge.* "And that proposition would be?" she asked.

"Control of Amora."

Marlena's attention became real in an instant.

"Partial control, of course... We'd still be behind you, *helping.*" Ryanna purred the last word, reminding Marlena of the act she was putting on—of the little secret they planned to keep from everyone. "Since you'll be so young, you'll need all the help you can get." She reminded Marlena that she would always be nothing but a puppet. "But you must take Ivelle under your wing. Help her stay out of trouble and learn that tarnishing an original name comes with consequences." Ryanna's eyes sparkled with unsaid words. Words she didn't have to say out loud for Marlena to hear.

She wanted Marlena to teach Ivelle to behave—just like she'd taught her.

Anger crept up her spine, a tingle of rage waking the part of her brain she wanted to keep dormant. *Take what you deserve.*

Ivelle scowled, ready to speak before Marlena held out a finger and silenced her.

"What are the requirements of this agreement?" Marlena asked, pinning Ivelle in her seat with nothing but the look on her face.

Celeste sighed, squeezing her daughter's shoulder, who ducked from her touch. Hurt rippled over Celeste's features. "I need Ivelle to learn poise, to learn her actions have serious repercussions." She never took her focus off Ivelle. "I have tried everything I can to get her to see she's hurting the people who love her, but it's not sticking." Her eyes watered. "I don't know what else to do. I'm desperate to break into that brain of hers."

Ivelle crossed her arms and sank further into her chair. It almost made Marlena chuckle, how bratty she was being. "There's nothing wrong with me. You're just overbearing and don't know when to leave me alone."

Celeste sighed, and her hurt was written in the lines of her face. "She's self-sabotaging."

*Control of Amora,* the little voice whispered. And for the first time ever, Marlena grinned at the words it hissed.

Accepting her parents' offer was a no-brainer. This was the start... and they couldn't keep her caged forever.

Her eyes locked on Ivelle, who met Marlena's stare with a matched coldness. "I accept your offer."

And when Marlena turned to her parents, she saw the exact moment a flash of worry for their decision caught them by surprise.

What kind of daughter had they raised?

Marlena's smile started at one corner of her mouth and snaked to the other side slowly. "When's my induction?"

*Okay, so I have to move to Amora.* This was worth it—no matter how cold and miserable she would be there... *it would be worth it.* Control of a territory at twenty-two years old would be worth it.

There had only been one other member who took over their seat at a younger age, and he still held it hundreds of years later. Nero wasn't a fighter—he was a fucking know-it-all who really did know it all. Sometimes, *nearly all the time,* it was insufferable. But Marlena knew it would be nice to have someone like him on her side.

When all of this blew up, she would need someone with millennia of knowledge willing to follow her around like a puppy afraid to get kicked by its owner. And he would when it came down to the end and he realized who was winning.

After hours of planning, Marlena finally left the meeting room for the first time. She was starving, really wanted a shower, and had been thinking about her night with Arlet any chance she got.

Marlena had to leave immediately, ready to take on the role of Fugere babysitter. Ivelle was in for a surprise if she thought she could walk all over Marlena.

No one would ever take advantage of her again.

The door to her room was ajar when she approached, and a maid scurried out with a few gowns draped over her arm.

All her things were gone, her room bare. Memories of nights she hadn't thought of in years flashed in her mind while the emptiness of the room consumed her.

How quickly had her parents wanted her washed clean from their home?

Marlena swallowed, spinning a circle until a maid interrupted the downward spiral she was nearing.

"Oh, Miss Marlena. I'm sorry. I was sent to grab the last of your wardrobe."

All she did was nod, watching as the woman quickly grabbed the last few dresses hanging in her closet.

And just like that, Marlena was removed from the Aeris home.

She wouldn't be taking over Amora until the first of the year. There were nearly ten months from now until the start of her rule, but she got the message loud and clear.

*Get out.* The unwanted voice didn't help ease the worry that her parents wouldn't stop here at erasing Marlena from their everyday lives.

They wanted her gone, but yet they wouldn't give her the full control she was rightfully entitled to by birth. Her parents would spend the rest of their lives dangling a carrot in front of Marlena, reminding her they were the ones who were really in control.

"Mar."

She spun around, eyes wide, as Vega came through the open door.

"What's going on?" Vega's eyebrows scrunched together as she cataloged the empty room.

There was no reason to be worried—this was the start of what she was born to do.

"I'm moving to Amora." Her voice sounded far away. "I get Amora. Mother's stepping down."

The silence of the room was no longer the sound ringing in Marlena's ears. It was now the sound of Vega's squeal and her feet against the floor as she jumped up and down with excitement.

Vega snatched her hands, and before Marlena knew it, they were jumping in circles like they were little girls again, playing games in the garden.

A laugh bubbled in the pit of her stomach as she stopped them before one, or both, got too dizzy and puked all over the nice, clean floor. "It's not happening until the beginning of the year, but apparently I have to move to Amora to help babysit our cousin."

"Ivelle?" Vega asked, confused.

Marlena shrugged. "She can't behave, and apparently I'm the person they think can change that."

Vega hummed, looking around the room again. "I don't know about that, but gods, did they clean your room out fast enough?" There was a bout of silence after Vega asked the question. Vega chuckled, trying to ease the tension tightening in the empty bedroom. "We should celebrate."

Marlena started to shake her head. "I—"

"Oh no, no, no. This is the moment you've been waiting your entire life for. You're not pulling that 'I have work to do' excuse tonight." Vega reached for her hand again, tugging her into the hall and leading her down the stairs to where Khort and Arlet were laid out on the couches in the sitting area.

"Yeah, but do you think they're ever going to stop rebelling? They don't *love* the idea of anything the Curia says they should do." Khort had his feet kicked up on the arm of a two-seater couch while he lay flat, throwing a palm-sized ball up in the air and waiting for it to fall back down to him.

Arlet was curled up, her feet tucked underneath her butt in a puffy chair. A blanket sat wrapped around her shoulders, covering the lounge clothes she somehow made look seamlessly flawless.

"Rebellions will happen until the people in charge squander them." Marlena joined, coming up behind the couch Khort was on. She leaned over, sticking her hand out at the right moment to snatch the ball from midair.

She could feel Arlet's eyes on her, and as much as she wanted to act cool, to lie to herself that she didn't care if Arlet was staring, Marlena caved. Her eyes dragged from the ball in her hand to Arlet. Khort grabbed for the ball, but Marlena made it disappear and chuckled when he grumbled about that "not being fair." She tossed the ball back, releasing her power and letting it reappear out of thin air seconds before it would have hit Khort in the head if he didn't have quick reflexes.

Marlena watched the way Arlet's eyes seemed to get heavy at the sight of her dress. When Marlena had gotten dressed this morning, she hadn't fully intended to pick something that would inherently drive Arlet wild... but she was glad she lucked out.

It seemed Arlet had always had a thing for boobs, but now Marlena was more apt to feel thankful for that nugget of information. She could tell it was true by the way Arlet bit her lip and turned her head to look out the window—like it was a job to force herself from ogling.

"We are not talking politics tonight," Vega declared, standing in the middle of the room with her hand on her hip. "We're celebrating."

"Celebrating what?" Arlet asked, her eyes jumping between Marlena and her sister.

"Mom's stepping down. Marlena gets Amora," Vega spewed, her excitement radiating warmth through the room.

Both Arlet and Khort shot up from their seats.

"No way!"

"Mar!"

And then everyone was screaming again. This time, Marlena controlled her emotions, masking a serious calmness. "Okay, okay, that's enough. It won't be happening for months, and I have to leave for Amora tonight."

"Fine." Arlet raced to the stairs and stopped on the first step. "Then we celebrate in Amora. Let me pack a bag."

Vega followed Arlet, her short legs taking the stairs two at a time, leaving Khort and Marlena alone for under five minutes before they came bounding back down the stairs with their overnight bags in tow.

They were welcomed with a late spring snowstorm upon their arrival to Amora. Not that it mattered if it was spring or not here—there would always be snow. *Always.* Marlena grumbled as they trudged up the buried walkway, but luckily, inside the home was warm.

For hours, the four sat around a fire, drinking spiked tea and laughing like old times. If Marlena focused hard enough, she could almost imagine what her life could have been like if it weren't for her parents' abuse... a life where she could simply laugh with her friends and truly celebrate her achievements.

Ivelle locked herself inside the room that was now hers, meaning Marlena didn't have to worry about her tonight.

A win.

One more night. She could have one more night before dealing with what her life was about to become.

The front door opened, and a draft of cold air followed Bridger in. He'd promised to meet them tonight, but the hours turned late, and no one expected him to make it with the shitty weather.

But it was becoming obvious there wasn't much that would keep Bridger from Vega—not even a nasty snowstorm.

Vega smiled across the room as Bridger shook the fat white flakes of snow out of his dark hair. "Good-fucking-luck with this snow all day, every day. Gods." He shivered, closing the distance between the door and where everyone sat around the sputtering fire. Khort was the furthest away, using whatever piece of his fire manifested outside his dragon form to keep warm.

Bridger mussed Marlena's hair as he walked by, and she swatted at his leg. "I hear congratulations are in order."

"Then just say them," Marlena grumbled, trying to fix her hair without a mirror.

Bridger plopped down next to Vega on the floor, where she'd been cuddled close to the fire all night like a lounging house cat.

For someone who had never been allowed around the other Curia children, Bridger had integrated nicely into their small circle. It was like he'd always been there.

Even Khort was starting to warm up to the idea of Bridger being around for the long haul.

Their conversation dragged on for a few more hours. Long enough for Vega to drift off to sleep, her head lying in Bridger's lap as he stroked her hair gently.

The snowstorm outside hadn't slowed, making it inconvenient for Khort to fly home tonight. So Khort and Arlet were going to share a room, while Bridger promised he would be fine on the plush rug by the fire.

Vega obviously had no issues sleeping, already snoring lightly in his lap.

Marlena was last to head to bed. She'd sat in the kitchen to finish the rest of her drink, watching the snow outside the massive picture window before hauling herself down the hall to her new bedroom with its creaky door.

She made a mental note to get it fixed tomorrow, but as soon as she turned around from shutting her door with a light *click*, that mental note flew out her brain and straight into the crackling fireplace keeping the room warm.

Arlet sat at the end of her bed in her pajamas, anxiously bouncing her leg. Her thigh jiggled, stealing some of Marlena's attention.

A slow smile spread across Marlena's lips. "This isn't the room you and Khort are sharing."

"I know, I..." Arlet stammered when meeting Marlena's piercing gaze. She licked her lips, eyes falling to Marlena's chest for a split second. "I don't want to stay with Khort."

She'd said it so quietly, Marlena almost thought she'd imagined the words. "Oh?" was all she could think to say.

"I wanted to—I don't know. I think I..." Arlet trailed off.

Marlena crossed the room, standing within an arm's distance of Arlet, who gazed at Marlena with a look she couldn't place.

"I wanted to congratulate you," Arlet said, letting out a breath.

The hairs on Marlena's neck stood, and she suppressed a chill. "You already have." Her voice matched Arlet's lightness.

"Not the way I want to."

Marlena couldn't move an inch, afraid if she did, it would spook Arlet. "And how do you want to congratulate me?"

Arlet's mouth opened, and then it closed... and then it opened again. And then it closed. It made the corner of Marlena's mouth stretch into a smile, which made Arlet groan. "Gods, I'm so lame. I came in here to take charge, to be spontaneous, to finally act on what I'm feeling. On what you're feeling. Or..." She paused. "What I *think* you're feeling, and then the longer I waited, the more I started to think maybe I'm crazy and last night we just got lost in the moment. But then I thought about the way you said goodbye to me this morning, and then I convinced myself it was a dream... but then the way you were looking at me tonight, it was like, *you knew*. Ya know?"

Marlena wasn't sure Arlet had taken a single breath while saying any of that. She didn't give her a moment to respond before she started again.

"And then this fucking dress." Arlet ran a hand down her face, exaggerating by biting her knuckle. "All night I was fighting for my fucking life trying to make eye contact with you instead of staring at your tits. Gods!" Arlet flopped back on the bed, her legs bent at the knees, hanging over the bed while she stared at the ceiling. "I can't even look at you. Please leave... your own room. I'm going to die of embarrassment."

Marlena knew she was joking, her tone keeping its low intensity. "Arlet."

She shook her head, arms draped over her face, covering her eyes.

Marlena's core burned, need building inside. "Arlet, I know."

That made Arlet sit up, her eyes wide. "You know?" The words only made sense to them, striking a match inside Marlena's gut.

Marlena dipped her head once, swallowing away the nerves. She was Marlena *fucking* Caelum, and she didn't get nervous. "How do you want to congratulate me, Arlet?" she asked again.

Arlet licked her lips. "Mar, I've never..." Her words trailed off.

"You've never?"

Arlet answered with a curt shake of her head. "Only with men."

Marlena's body made a decision before her brain caught up. She dropped to her knees on the floor, hands resting on Arlet's thighs. "What do you want?" The bed was the perfect height to bury herself between Arlet's legs. Marlena bit down on her lip hard at the realization.

Arlet's throat tightened when she swallowed. "Kiss me."

It was all the permission Marlena needed. She reached up and grabbed the back of Arlet's head, wrapping her fingers in her curls, and brought their lips together.

*So soft.* Arlet was so soft.

Marlena's free hand trailed up her exposed skin, tiny chill-bumps forming underneath her fingertips. Her lips parted, and her tongue slid over Arlet's plump bottom lip. Marlena sucked it into her mouth for a second before releasing and trailing kisses down her chin, then underneath her jaw, until she couldn't reach anymore and was forced to pull away.

Arlet arched back, pressing her chest out, and her breathing turned ragged. The strap on her left shoulder fell down, Arlet's amber skin glowing against the fire in the hearth of the small bedroom. The room was nearly half the size of the one she had in Aeris.

The home in Amora was big, but it felt like a cabin with its creaky floors and poorly lit rooms.

But Marlena wasn't fucking thinking about how much she hated this house right now...

It wasn't long before Marlena's lips found something else to connect with, and she was pulling Arlet by the crooks of her knees until her ass was at the edge of the mattress.

Marlena kissed Arlet's thighs, hands sliding under her top. She took both of Arlet's breasts in her hands at the same time and squeezed, Arlet's nipples pebbling under her touch.

"Tell me if you want me to stop." Marlena's voice was breathless as she inhaled the sweet scent of Arlet's skin. *Honey. She always smells like fresh, sweet honey.* One hand dropped down, fiddling with the waistband of her shorts. The other stayed to roll her nipple between her fingers.

"Don't." The word fell from Arlet's lips in a moan, soaking Marlena between her thighs. She wiggled on her knees, rubbing her legs together to ease the ache.

Arlet's hazel eyes were heavy and half-lidded with lust, sending Marlena into a frenzy. Marlena kissed her way up, spreading Arlet's legs apart until her lips lingered over the outside of her shorts, damp with Arlet's desire.

Marlena's eyes rolled into the back of her head at the way Arlet peered down at her, like she was begging Marlena to go farther. "Fuck, Arlet. I need to taste you." With one swift pull, Marlena tore her out of her shorts and tossed them to the side.

And the sight lying before her had Marlena drawing in a breath, swallowing the drool fighting to escape from her watering mouth. Arlet, bare, with nothing to get in the way. "So pretty. So fucking pretty." Marlena parted Arlet's legs wider, running a thumb over the lips of her pussy.

Arlet wiggled her hips, pressing into Marlena's finger, incoherent whimpers coming out on heavy breaths.

Marlena gave in to her need, pushing her thumb between Arlet's wet lips. She swirled her finger in slow circles over her clit, putting just the right amount of pressure to send Arlet plopping down onto her back. Her back arched, knees bending as her heels dug into the bed. Instinctively, Marlena took her free arm and looped it through Arlet's leg to hold her in place. Her fingers lightly trailed over the skin of her hipbone.

Marlena had branched out since her one night with the unknown Ardor-born, taking the time to explore new lovers. Everyone knew Marlena was a perfectionist, and sex was no exception.

She knew her way around a bedroom and was prepared to show Arlet exactly what she was capable of.

"Be a good girl and hold still," Marlena purred, sliding a single finger inside Arlet, and then finally, *finally*, she sank between her thighs.

Marlena ran her tongue from Arlet's hole to her clit in one long, deliberate line, getting her first taste. She twisted her finger, sliding one more in before pressing against her soft spot deep inside and sucking Arlet's clit between her lips.

Arlet mewled, body writhing. Marlena didn't let up on the movement of her fingers, but her eyes fluttered to watch Arlet playing with her nipples. Her hips bucked when Marlena gently nibbled on her clit, and she gasped.

Releasing Arlet from her mouth, Marlena hummed against the inside of her leg. "Shhh, don't wake the whole house, pet." The nickname rolled off her tongue without a second thought.

"Marlena, gods. You're so good. That's so good," Arlet whined, sitting up on her forearms to watch while Marlena sank back between her thighs with a hunger she'd never felt before. She sucked Arlet's clit back into her mouth and slammed her fingers as far in as they could go, finding a rhythm that seemed to bring Arlet to the edge. Watching Arlet come undone after months of tiptoeing around what they were feeling was euphoric.

Arlet's head fell back, and she bit her lip hard to contain a moan that hummed in her throat. Marlena couldn't help but watch the way Arlet unraveled for her.

"So tight. Fuck, you're so tight and wet for me." Her breath washed over Arlet's clit, and it was like her words hit a trigger because Arlet's stomach tightened and her legs began to quiver. Marlena held tight to keep her in place.

"Mar, I'm gonna come. Right there," Arlet gasped. "Right there, ohhhmygooodsssss." Her eyes fluttered, and her already snug walls clenched around Marlena's fingers.

Her pussy pulsed while Marlena continued to finger her through the pleasure, enjoying the sweet taste of Arlet's release coating her tongue. Marlena pulled her fingers out, lightly stroking Arlet's clit as she used her other hand to wipe the combination of Arlet's cum and her saliva from her chin. She savored the taste.

Arlet watched Marlena with a heavy gaze, her bottom lip trapped between her teeth until she spoke. "Let me taste."

Marlena plunged her fingers back inside her pussy, watching her gasp from the sudden intrusion. "You wanna taste how sweet you are?"

A sweet moan vibrated against Arlet's lips, her hips rolling against Marlena's hand.

Marlena wasn't sure she'd ever be able to get the noises Arlet made out of her head.

Arlet nodded, the nerves she'd worn earlier peeling away.

Marlena pushed off the floor, pulling her fingers out and stepping in between Arlet's legs. She had to crane her neck to look at Marlena, but her lips parted, and she reached up to take Marlena's fingers into her mouth. The warmth of her tongue twirling around Marlena's fingers made her rub her legs together, seeking friction for herself.

The way Arlet's tongue slid between Marlena's fingers, making sure she cleaned every bit of herself off, had Marlena sinking to her knees on top of Arlet, straddling her lap.

Arlet didn't take Marlena's fingers out of her mouth as she scooted back to give Marlena more room on the bed.

Marlena pulled them out herself with a *pop* from the suction. Her hand fell to Arlet's face, thumb and pointer finger settling underneath her chin to guide her lips to hers. Arlet instantly opened her mouth, inviting Marlena inside, and the taste of her release lingered on their tongues.

Marlena was used to fighting for power, inside and outside of the bedroom, but Arlet melted under her touch, allowing her to do what she pleased while her hands cupped Marlena's breasts through her dress.

Her grip was light at first, until Marlena pressed into her touch, silently begging for more.

Arlet pulled away from their kiss, running her hands down Marlena's body. "I want to see you. All of you. Take this off." She gathered the skirt of her dress around her hips, and Marlena reached behind to unclip the belt around her torso. Her tits bounced to their natural resting place, still perky and full. Marlena hadn't worried about a bra today, suddenly happy she'd forgone one.

Arlet tugged the dress over Marlena's head, and the soft fabric against her skin sent chills throughout her body, leaving her in nothing but a pair of lacy panties that didn't cover much of her ass. "Gods." Arlet exhaled, her hands back on Marlena's bare chest.

Marlena's breathing hitched as Arlet's thumbs brushed over her nipples, rubbing small circles over them until they were beaded.

Arlet leaned forward, taking one in her mouth as she pinched at the other. Her tongue flicked over the sensitive skin, causing Marlena to sink into Arlet's lap further, grinding against her thigh. "Fuck."

Her lips suckled on Marlena's sensitive bud. Arlet looked up at her, grazing her teeth over with a light nibble. "Teach me how to touch you. I want to make you feel good. I want to make you come."

Marlena trembled under her touch as a hand slid between her legs, chills running down her back. "Show me how you touch yourself." Her hand shot down to guide Arlet's where she wanted it.

Arlet didn't hesitate. She moved Marlena's underwear to the side and slid a finger in between her lips. "Oh, you're soaked." She bit her lip, swirling around Marlena's opening. "Drenched." She plunged her finger inside, making Marlena rock her hips and groan softly when her clit rubbed against Arlet's palm.

"One more," Marlena ordered against Arlet's lips, kissing her like she couldn't get enough. A second finger added, Marlena gripped Arlet's shoulders, letting one hand trail to the back of her head, where she tangled her hand in her curly hair. She forced Arlet to lock eyes with her. There was a look of hunger on Arlet's face, her eyes swimming with desire. Arlet's fingers moved inside Marlena while she rubbed the heel of her palm into her clit. "Yes, just like that," Marlena purred.

"You're so hot. Gods, I wish you could see yourself right now." Arlet broke the distance between their lips, crashing hers against Marlena's and capturing her next moan.

Marlena had to pull away from her lips, panting from the

pleasure and unable to focus on anything other than the way Arlet found the spot inside her like she'd done this a million times before. "Play with my nipples." Her hand fell from Arlet's hair, dropping back to her shoulders.

Arlet took direction well, wasting no time flicking her tongue over Marlena's hard nipple. She rotated between each, giving them equal attention.

Her pleasure came in like a crashing wave, sending bolts of ecstasy to her core. Marlena had to continue to remind herself this home wasn't big enough to make too much noise with all its visitors tonight.

Marlena's body started to tingle with her impending orgasm. She threw her head back, pushing into Arlet's mouth with her chest. "Yes, yes. I'm so close." Her bright blonde hair fell behind her shoulders, the feel of it tickling her back sending her over the edge.

Tumbling.

Falling.

Plunging.

She had to bite her lip hard enough to taste blood to keep herself from screaming. The moan rumbled in her chest, her whole body tightening as her body ruptured with pleasure.

Marlena's quieted moans vibrated down her throat, and Arlet let go of her nipple to kiss up her neck. "That's the hottest thing I've ever seen. Fuck." She kept her fingers moving, letting Marlena ride out the rest of her orgasm.

Marlena's chest rose in sharp inhales, and she felt like she was fluttering down from another world. Her whole body sang with release.

Arlet slipped her fingers out and immediately brought them to her lips, lapping up Marlena's cum. "You taste better than I imagined you could."

Finally able to form a coherent thought, Marlena smiled lazily and leaned in to lick what was left of herself off Arlet's lips. "Next time I'll teach you how to go down on me so you can really get a good taste."

Marlena slid off Arlet's lap, and they both collapsed beside each other. Their heavy breathing and the crackling fire were the only sounds in the room until Arlet broke their silence. "So, there's gonna be a next time then, huh?"

Smiling devilishly, Marlena turned her head. "Give me three minutes to catch my breath, and I'll make sure you're a pro by the time you leave my room in the morning."

Arlet didn't wait, springing to her knees, positioning herself over Marlena. "How about you lie there, and I'll get started early?"

Without hesitation, Arlet sank between Marlena's thighs. Her body shuddered from the sensitivity of her last orgasm.

Marlena grabbed a handful of the comforter as Arlet effortlessly brought her to another climax and thought to herself, *I'm fucked.*

## Twenty-One Years Old

THE HOUSE WAS EMPTY OF EVERYONE BUT IVELLE WHEN Marlena finally rolled out of bed and freshened up for the day.

It had been a long night. One where neither Arlet nor Marlena got a wink of sleep before she snuck out and left with Khort.

When they'd heard him stir, his heavy steps echoing down the hall, Arlet slipped out with the lie that she'd fallen asleep on the couch in Marlena's office after finding a book to read.

Arlet never read books...

Ivelle sat at the kitchen table with a danish and a cup of tea, watching the snow that had continued overnight.

"Good morning." Marlena stood at the island, eyeing Ivelle as one of the maids poured her a cup of tea.

Ivelle didn't turn around, ignoring her. And to no one's surprise, that sent a fireball of anger roaring through Marlena.

Marlena's wind shot from her body like tendrils, rushing around the room and pushing Ivelle's chair back with a loud screech from the legs grinding against the floor. Ivelle's eyes grew wide, searching for Marlena, but she was gone.

She dropped the cloak of her invisibility, bending at the waist to meet Ivelle at eye level. "It's insanely rude to ignore someone in their own home. In the home you now live in, mind you." Marlena stared into her green eyes, watching Ivelle try to school her features into neutrality.

"What the fuck is your problem?" Ivelle asked, doing a good job at pretending she wasn't flustered.

Marlena painted a pretty smile on her face, standing up straight. "You and your bad attitude. You're acting like a child. No one would ever believe you're, what? Four years older than I am? You should be grateful I'm willing to take you in."

Ivelle barked a laugh laced with venom. "I should be grateful? No, more like *you* should be grateful." Ivelle stood, not quite as tall as Marlena but tall enough to look her dead in the eye. "If it weren't for me, you wouldn't be getting Amora this early."

Marlena's teeth ground together so hard they might shatter to bits. "If it weren't for me taking you in like a lost fucking puppy, you'd have nowhere else to go. It's clear your mother is at her wits' end with you, and your father didn't even show up to your own relegation." Marlena raised a brow. "What's that about?"

"You know nothing about me, Marlena. You know nothing of what I've been through." Ivelle was beautiful, with wavy red hair reaching the small of her back and green eyes the color of a blooming garden in spring. All her facial features were soft, her cheekbones round, her nose the perfect slope. Everything about her was Amora-born. "While you and your sister got handed everything you ever wanted, some of us were left in the dark, being stripped of what was rightfully ours." A fire burned behind her eyes, its embers built off years of resentment.

*She sounds just like me.* A languid, bubbling laugh erupted from Marlena's stomach. If only someone could have laid witness to what she'd endured as a child—up until a few years ago, Marlena was still wearing daily bruises from her parents' *love.*

Ivelle stood still as can be, watching Marlena until she caught her breath.

"That's a good one." Marlena's smile fell from her face without warning, and she stepped in close to Ivelle again, crowding her space. "I want you to listen to me, loud and clear, you got it?" Of course Ivelle didn't move, but that didn't rattle Marlena. "You're not going to assume anything about me. You're not going to pretend you know how I was raised or what I had to do to get where I am now."

Marlena had lost parts of herself. What would she have been like if her parents weren't her parents... if she'd been born into another life?

If they had loved her like they loved Vega...

"If you wanted the seat so badly, you should've tried to take it." Marlena cocked her head to the side, feeling like a snake about to strike. "Instead, you turned into a spoiled fucking brat who's never done anything but sulk in what was never meant to be yours."

Ivelle's muscles were taut and it almost looked like she wasn't breathing.

"Your new job is to listen to me. That's it. Nothing else." Marlena wouldn't take the first step back. She waited for Ivelle, who hadn't decided she was ready to budge yet but who wasn't saying anything anymore either. "You are here because no one else wants you. Kind of like me. So if you think that for one second, you're going to come in here and out-trauma me and make me feel bad for you, you are sadly mistaken."

Ivelle let out a breath and took a tiny step back.

"Now, should we try this again?" Marlena gestured to the chair Ivelle had been sitting in. "Good morning, Ivelle." Her voice was quiet, returning to a normal decibel.

Through a still-clenched jaw, Ivelle sat while holding Marlena's gaze. "Good morning." Her tone was the grumble of a scolded teenager.

Marlena grabbed her mug off the table and looked over her shoulder from the doorway. "We're hosting the Curia meeting tonight to make the announcement of my succession. Be ready by four-thirty."

*If they won't listen, make them.*

Twenty-One Years Old

It had been weeks since Marlena had a single moment to sit down, and it didn't look like it would be slowing anytime soon.

She touched up her makeup in Vega's bedroom, where her sister was sprawled on the bed. "Do you ever wonder where the gods went when they died? Like, what ever happened to Pluto and the underworld? Do you think he got left behind on Earth or something?" Vega stared at the ceiling, her eyes watching the fan spin.

"Are you high?" she asked, avoiding making direct eye contact with herself in the mirror. It had been twelve years since she'd spent six days locked inside the room full of mirrors, but that time alone still haunted her.

"No, but I did start thinking about it last week after I tried unregulated ale from Fraus."

Marlena popped her lips, evening her lipstick out. "You know if our parents catch you, you're going to be in trouble."

Vega laughed and pushed herself onto her elbows. "I'm nineteen. They can't control my every move."

*Yes, they can. They are. They will.*

"What are they gonna do? Kick me out? I'll just come live with you." None of Vega's worries were real—none of her plans were forced on her. She'd been able to do whatever she wanted, whenever she wanted.

Marlena finally turned to look at her sister. "I mean, what is your plan? You can't just dream about other worlds for the rest of your life. You need to find a purpose, something you can work towards." *So you don't end up as nothing but a baby-making machine.*

Vega curled her legs underneath her. "I don't know." She shrugged. "I don't think I have a plan. I know I want to help people... those less fortunate than us. Maybe stop the resistance happening in the territories."

Marlena really struggled to contain her eye roll, but she did. "That's very noble of you, Vega, but I don't think you're going to be able to have any say in that."

Vega got that look on her face when she was ready to defend her point. "I disagree. Bridger and I talk about it all the time. What he's going to be able to do when he takes over as commander. All the good he can bring. He wants to change the way the army is run, give people a home who have never felt wanted."

Somewhere deep in Marlena's chest, there was a pang of guilt and a smidge of sadness for the world her sister dreamed of...

It wasn't the world that would win in the end.

This wasn't a fairytale.

This was the real world. One where the princesses didn't get to keep their princes and no one lived happily ever after.

She wanted to be gentle with Vega, but she also wanted to prepare her for what was to come. "You know they're never going to let you stay with him, right?"

Vega's eyebrows scrunched. "What do you mean?"

*Sometimes the truth hurts.* Her mother's voice had been quieter these days, but it wasn't gone—it had just turned into something else... something more that Marlena was fighting to keep out.

"He's destined for a different path than you. Our parents know that. Everyone knows that. They're not going to follow our parents if this resistance goes south." And it would; *it will.*

Vega hadn't moved from the bed, but her posture stiffened. "Why do you think it's going to get bad? You're going to be leading a territory soon. You get to be their voice, the one who stands up if things go bad."

*Naive.*

"I just don't want to see you get hurt." Marlena couldn't tell her about her alliances. Not yet. There was still too much she needed to do, but she held out hope that when it all crumbled, her sister would pick her. Marlena would finally let her in on the secrets she kept... but not yet, not when their parents were still breathing down her neck, waiting for their chance to snatch her up. "And he's going to hurt you. His father has said so himself. He'll get bored—"

Vega jumped off the bed, a grumble leaving her chest that sounded like a mad jungle cat. "Yeah, yeah, he'll get bored of me. That's what they all say! That's what everyone, every single person, is saying. You don't think I've heard the whispers when we're together? Heard the things his own parents have said when they don't think I can hear them?" She pointed at her chest. "I'm not the right one." Vega started listing off all the hurtful things she'd heard. "Marlena would bring more opportunities to bridge the gap between territories. What does the little sister have to offer? The other Caelum girl is prettier." Vega snatched a sweater off the back of a chair and stomped to the door. "Do you think I don't know that no one wants us together? That everyone is aware that I was promised to someone well before I got the chance to make that decision for myself? That I'm hurting my best friend in the process? All because I fell in love... I know you think my problems are trivial compared to what you deal with, but they're still my problems, my worries."

Vega opened the door to her room, ready to shut Marlena out. "I want to see a world where the Vegas and Bridgers can fall in love without anyone questioning if they're worthy of each other."

The door shut, leaving Marlena alone.

The fear of being alone was once something of the past, but the loneliness was sinking back in with bigger fangs this time.

*You're always going to be alone.*

Part of Marlena's deal was that she took Ivelle under her wing, showing her what being a proper lady was all about—a proper lady who could be married off to someone with money or an impressive ability—in the hope Ivelle could become a meek housewife... the same they hoped for Vega.

Marlena hadn't seen Vega since she'd stormed out of her room. Bridger and Khort were at the weekly meeting, and they hadn't acted any different than they did—maybe Vega had stormed off to cool down.

Her fingers were crossed this would all blow over; no need to fix what wasn't broken.

Marlena exited the meeting room as soon as it was over, followed by Bridger and Khort. Ivelle sat slumped in a chair in the waiting area, the most childish pout creasing her usually pretty face. "You've got to be sick of acting this way." Marlena crossed her arms, popping a hip.

Ivelle, as to be expected, stood and stomped off down the hall like a fucking toddler.

Marlena sighed, throwing her head back to stare at the ceiling while she took another deep breath before righting herself and following the boys down the hallway.

"She needs a tranquilizer," Bridger joked, watching Ivelle disappear. "Khort, got anything back home that'll calm her down?"

Khort's laugh was sarcastic, but it was nice to see him opening up to Bridger more lately—it wasn't his fault he'd won Vega's heart. Khort turned and walked backwards because he knew the halls of the Aeris home like they were his own. "You staying here tonight?" he asked Marlena. "Since Bridger is here, we figured we'd get some late-night training in."

"No, I think it's time I get Ivelle home before she blows this whole place up with her disdain."

Bridger paused at the stairs. "What's her problem?" He rested his hand on the banister.

Marlena sneered. "Everything is her problem."

The sound of footsteps echoed up the staircase, and before she saw them, she knew who it would be.

Vega and Arlet met them at the top, and Marlena's eyes only stayed on her sister for a moment before they caught Arlet's. Vega was too busy giving Bridger a hello kiss, and Khort was too busy pretending he wasn't crawling out of his skin, to notice the smile Arlet saved just for Marlena.

*She sees me.*

They were still meeting in private when they could, but it had been almost a week and Marlena was craving her touch.

"Headed out?" Vega asked, not doing a great job hiding her aggravation.

Bridger honed in on it immediately, his eyes bouncing between the sisters. He didn't say anything, but he was watching, waiting for Marlena's response.

"Yes" was all Marlena could muster up. If Vega wanted to tell her friends they were fighting, she could do it herself. Marlena had other things to worry about.

Arlet leaned against the banister, a few steps down. "Why don't you stay?"

*Fuck.*

Marlena had to look away. Arlet had those *please fuck me* eyes and there was no way she could say no if she kept staring like that.

"Not tonight." She squeezed past Bridger and Vega on the top step. "Babysitting my bratty cousin is a full-time job, apparently."

The stairwell led to the kitchen, allowing access to the help when the meeting room turned into a dining room during late-night councils.

Marlena might have intentionally walked a little closer than she needed to Arlet, their hands brushing as Marlena continued to descend the stairs.

Her skin tingled where Arlet had touched, and her mind was lost in it until she was alone in the long hallway leading to the kitchen, where she could focus on other things besides Arlet's feverous touch.

"Ivelle, why must you make everything so difficult?" The Aeris home was large, with many rooms Ivelle could have slipped into, unnoticed.

Marlena searched the first few rooms off the long hallway, and to her dismay, Ivelle wasn't in any of them. The next room went into the wine cellar. *I should take a couple bottles home... might make it easier to deal with her.*

She opened the door and called down the spiral staircase, "Ivelle! You have literal seconds before I start to lose my cool." A pair of footsteps bounded down the hallway, pulling her attention away from the cellar. "Gods, thank you. It gets old scolding you like a child all the ti—" Marlena turned the corner and was met with Arlet, her lips immediately finding hers. She pinned her against the hallway wall, straddling her thigh to get her body as close to Marlena as she could. She was the one with the position to take control, but she still let Marlena lead.

Her hands trailed up the sides of Arlet's body. Marlena grabbed a handful of her ass, earning a gasp against her lips.

Anyone could come through and catch them. A thrill of excitement crept up her spine, and Marlena wouldn't have cared about being caught if it were anyone other than Arlet.

What would they think? Marlena, with the powerless one...

Marlena still let her hands roam over Arlet's curves, but she pulled away from her mouth, kissing down the slope of her jaw. "Is this you trying to convince me to stay?"

*I could.*

Arlet leaned her head back, grinding against Marlena's leg between her thighs. "Is it working?" she panted.

"Aw, pet. You're extra needy tonight, aren't you?" Marlena nibbled on her earlobe.

Arlet inhaled sharply. "I need you. Been needing you so badly. Thinking about you between my legs all week." Her words were breathy, hinting at just how desperate she was for Marlena.

She grabbed Arlet by the face, squeezing her cheeks to push her lips into a pout. "Want me to get you off so you can stop thinking about me?"

Arlet shook her head as best as she could in Marlena's grasp. "I don't want to stop thinking about you. I want you to stay so I get my taste too." She ground her hips again, this time with more pressure and need. Marlena knew if she reached a hand between Arlet's thighs, she would be *soaked*.

"I think I like the idea of you touching yourself in bed tonight when I'm not there to give you your fix." Marlena kissed her puckered lips greedily.

"Marlena."

Arlet startled at the voice, retreating away from Marlena until her back pressed against the opposite wall.

Marlena wiped her lips, fixed her dress, and turned to face their interruption. "Now you choose to show up."

Arlet was flustered, her eyes wide with worry. They'd been caught red-handed by Ivelle—Ivelle, who had reason to turn Marlena's life upside down if she pleased.

Marlena schooled herself into calmness, pushing away whatever tension she felt. "I'll meet you outside. Don't make me come looking for you again." She pointed towards the front of the house where their vehicle would be waiting to take them to Fortis's docks.

Traveling to Marlena's new home was a fucking *pain*.

Ivelle eyed them both, her arms crossed like she might put up a fight. Instead, she turned and left the hallway, leaving Marlena and Arlet alone again.

Arlet shook her head, doing her best not to freak out—but Marlena could see through her attempt at masking her nerves. "I— Mar, I'm so sorry. I shouldn't have... Oh gods, what if she outs us?"

Her reaction struck a chord inside Marlena, but not one of understanding, even though moments before she'd been concerned about the same thing. One that made her speculate why this was Arlet's response to people finding out about them. "Why are you so worried?"

Arlet's brows drew together like the answer was obvious. "Why wouldn't I be? After what you said about your parents today to Vega, how they don't want her to be with Bridger... What makes you think they'd be okay with us together? The powerless Videri doesn't stand a chance at being the right match for their soon-to-be seat holder daughter if Bridger, future Commander Dimico, can't be for Vega."

There was so much she didn't understand—so much Marlena couldn't tell her yet. *It's not time.* She ran a hand down her face, the only sign her temper was rising. "Arlet, I can't do this right now. I have to go." She gestured towards where Ivelle had gone. "I'll see you soon, okay?"

A flash of hurt washed over Arlet's face, her shoulders sagging with an abrupt exhale, and for the briefest of seconds, Marlena considered staying—letting Ivelle wait outside all night if she needed to.

But she couldn't.

Marlena peeled her eyes off Arlet and left her standing in the hall, hopeful she wouldn't mope for too long.

They could talk about this later.

They could figure it out. *Later*.

For now, Marlena had to make sure Ivelle knew who she was messing with.

Maybe they could tell people about them... eventually. But they had to do it the right way, and Arlet had to be let in.

All the way in.

And Marlena wasn't sure she'd ever be able to let her get that close.

She stormed out into the humid night air, walking on light feet. Marlena used the power of her wind to stifle the sound of her footsteps.

Ivelle didn't hear her coming until Marlena's fingernails dug into the flesh of her bicep and she shoved her toward their vehicle. Ivelle tried to snatch her arm from Marlena's clutch, but that only made Marlena dig in deeper.

"Let go," she shouted, trying to squirm out of Marlena's grip.

Marlena doubled down, clutching her tighter, and sent a rough breeze through the trees surrounding the Aeris property to cover the sound of her demands.

"Get in the fucking vehicle, Ivelle," Marlena growled, pushing her forward with enough force she stumbled on her feet, barely catching herself before connecting with the hard exterior of the military transport.

Ivelle spun around, ready to strike Marlena before she disappeared and stepped out of her way. She reappeared as she spoke. "I'll let that one slide, but the next time you think about raising a hand to me, it better be a killing blow, because I won't show this kindness again."

Ivelle was a spoiled brat Dand had never once been given a single fucking rule to follow. Or at least, she'd never listened to one.

*That changes now.*

The soldier jobbed in taking them to the Fortis docks flinched, flustered as he momentarily struggled to pull the door open for the girls.

"You have some nerve, thinking you can boss me around after what I just saw!" Ivelle's voice was a piercing screech, scraping against Marlena's eardrums like a dying bird.

"I'm going to give you three fucking seconds."

Maybe it was something in Marlena's eyes, or the fact that she held up a finger and started counting, but before she could get to three, Ivelle ducked into the cab of their transport.

The door clicked shut, and Marlena didn't wait another second to lay into her. "I am only going to say this once... What you saw tonight is none of your fucking business, and I promise, *I swear* to every dead god and any that come next, I will make your life a living hell if you utter a single breath to anyone." Marlena didn't feel the transport move, her gaze stuck on Ivelle and the sneer painted on her lips.

"Do you think your threats scare me?" Marlena knew they did sometimes—she'd seen the way Ivelle responded to her powers in the kitchen.

"Oh, I'm sorry... Did you think that was a threat?" Marlena leaned against her plush bench, oozing nonchalance. "I've been making threats my whole life. It's time for me to make good on them, turn them into promises. If you wanted someone to walk all over, you're a few years late. That Marlena is dead."

*I killed her.*

Ivelle hadn't settled into her seat. She sat rigid, every muscle in her body fighting the coolness she was trying to hold on to... Marlena could see the crack, could tell she was close to breaking.

"Nothing you can do to me will be worse than what I've lived through. Why would you want to keep Arlet a secret? If it's such a big deal, maybe it's information that will earn me my freedom back. Maybe even earn me the seat that I was robbed of." Ivelle shrugged her shoulders, finally sinking into her seat with a smug smirk on her pink-painted lips.

She thought she'd won.

Marlena leaned forward, taking up the space between them with her elbows resting on her knees. "What have you done to deserve my seat? The seat I've fought for, bled for, given up parts of myself I'll never get back for. All you've done is make a fool of yourself, make yourself look like the last person they'd let lead. I bet they'd give it to Vega over you. As a matter of fact, I *know* they would." Marlena's voice dripped with pity. "And then you'd have nothing. No one on your side, no one to align yourself with when the world you know burns to the fucking ground."

Ivelle raised a brow. "What?"

"Oh, so now you're curious?" Marlena wanted Ivelle to understand the position they were in. For it to really sink in that Marlena was, in fact, the only person left who could give her what she wanted.

There was a fight in her... a girl who just wanted to get a taste of what power felt like. "I am the only person left who can give you what you want, Ivelle, and I would hate for you to ruin that by running your mouth like this is some schoolyard." Marlena relaxed, crossing one long leg over the other. "I've had enough of the abuse our lineage thinks is normal, and I plan on making them regret it soon enough."

Marlena caught the exact moment she hooked her.

Another line set.

Ivelle's eyes lit up, a twinkle of hope and understanding dawning.

"All you have to do is play by my rules, and I'll make sure you get everything you've ever wanted." Marlena twirled her wrist. "Within reason."

Ivelle spoke quietly. "And how do I know I can trust you? That this isn't some test our mothers set up to see how I'd respond?"

"Are you really willing to trust our mothers over me?" Marlena raised a perfectly shaped brow, watching Ivelle's head shake side to side very, very slowly. "If you don't pick me, who's going to protect you when I make good on all my promises? We both know it won't be our mothers, and I don't think you've got an ally in your back pocket that I don't know about, do you?" A slow smile spread across her face. "I have all the allies we need. I just need you to act like nothing is happening, to act like I fixed you, and if you can do that, if you can fall in line behind me, I'll give you Amora."

*Because I won't need the cold fucking hellscape when I'm finished with it anyway.*

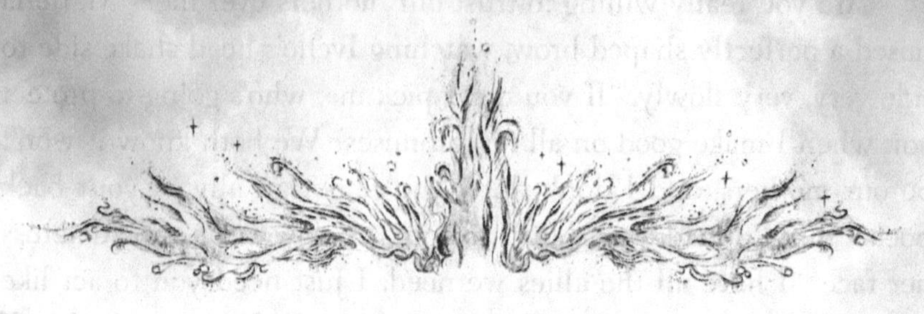

## Twenty-One Years Old

"I think at this point, if there's an alliance being formed, we should all be a part of the decision-making. Bringing in strangers right now could be risky, don't you think?" Zetta's tone wasn't harsh—it was borderline endearing.

Marlena rolled her eyes, pushing herself off the desk she'd been leaning against. "I don't need permission to bring anyone into the alliance I have created." Her eyes scanned over the people in the room. Zetta and her husband, Miklov, stood side by side. Miklov usually stayed quiet, allowing his wife to do all the talking. After all, she was the Curia member, not him.

Dacian Viator stood by himself, keeping his distance. Frausborns tended to watch out for themselves, and only themselves. "We have been at this a lot longer than you, girl."

Marlena spun quickly, a snarl on her lips. "Yes, and you've done a great job doing nothing up until now." Everything they'd done had never worked. Their lineage had always been failures when it came to the important parts.

Lucius and Katrin shared a glance before Lucius spoke. "We haven't really been doing nothing, maybe biding our time, but we have people ready to take what is rightfully theirs."

"Perfect. As do I." Marlena motioned to Ivelle, who was sitting with her long legs draped over the edge of the desk Marlena had been leaning on. She twirled a piece of her long auburn hair, raising a brow and letting the hair fall back into place to wiggle her fingers in a snarky hello.

Their conversation after Ivelle caught her and Arlet together had been a week ago, and things had started to settle between the two. While they weren't ready to spill their deepest, darkest secrets, something Marlena would probably never do anyway, they were at least beginning to figure out exactly what they both wanted.

Just last night, they had been standing in the hall before going to their bedrooms. Ivelle stopped before twisting the doorknob to her room, turned to Marlena, and said, "I don't want my mother to survive whatever it is you have planned."

But would she be willing to kill her herself? And how far was Marlena willing to go?

Death wasn't a line she'd crossed yet, but she knew she would.

She could.

*I will. To get what I want, I'll do worse.*

Marlena looked around the room, catching the eye of a passerby through the open door. *Who the fuck didn't close it?* And why had she just now noticed?

Khort hesitated for a second, their eyes locked on one another's. Before he continued his forward motion, his eyes scanned the rest of the people standing around the room... and then he disappeared.

Marlena cursed under her breath. "You are all a bunch of fucking idiots. If you can't trust me, then I don't see why you're still here." Before she slipped through the threshold, she turned and said loudly enough that the people in the room were the only ones to hear her, "We strike on my induction night. Everyone will be distracted by the party. Start preparing."

Two months. She had two months to figure out her exact plan. Two months to tell Vega. Arlet. Khort.

*Fuck, Khort.*

She slipped from the room and quieted her feet with the air

around her, making sure Khort didn't hear her coming up until she was right beside him.

He jumped, gasping in a sharp breath. "Gods, Marlena. You really need to stop doing that. It's freaky."

Marlena hummed what might be considered a laugh, turning the corner with him. "Where ya going?"

Khort side-eyed her, slowing his pace. "Dinner with my parents and Delori."

They were all in Fortis today, preparing for the next recruitment of soldiers for the army. Marlena had asked for more protection around her home in Amora. After the announcement of her succession and the introduction of Ivelle as her second, much to her own parents' dismay, there could be backlash—people didn't always agree with who was next in line to lead. "You can't be too careful," she'd said when her parents shot daggers her way for making decisions without consulting them.

Khort's parents had him around over the last few years for different things, teaching him slowly about all the ins and outs of what running a territory looked like... and today was both of their first times seeing the way Lucius ran his army from the frontline.

He was fucking brutal.

A great ally, but not someone Marlena would give her full trust to.

"Some recruitment today, huh?" Marlena asked, making small talk. She had to know what he'd heard.

Thankfully, he didn't take long to break.

"Yeah." Khort stopped, turning to Marlena. "Why were you in there talking to them?"

Fraus, Fortis, and Ardor weren't to be trusted. That was what they'd all been taught growing up. *Watch your backs. Don't get too close to anyone you meet.*

Khort eyed her suspiciously.

Marlena's eyebrows met in the middle, and she molded herself into the person she needed to be for him to believe her. "Oh." She looked behind her, waving her hand in the direction of the room she'd exited. "That? We were just talking about the guards coming to Amora with me and Ivelle."

Khort studied her as if he was trying to catch her in a lie, but he wouldn't see any cracks. Marlena would never crack again. "So why were Zetta and Dacian in there then?"

Marlena didn't have to think about the lie too deeply. "Because I barged in on them. I wanted to make sure I was going home with the guards I requested. Now that the news of my induction has been announced and people know Ivelle is with me, I wouldn't want anyone to lash out. With the uprisings I don't want anyone thinking this is a good moment to attack, to come after us when we're alone."

People had lashed out during the transfer of power before. It didn't happen often, but it did happen. Some people had nothing to lose.

She watched Khort rest and take in a deep breath. He believed her. "You need to be careful with them, Marlena. You can't just insert yourself anywhere. These people, *those people*, aren't interested in helping you. If anything, they're probably more interested in taking advantage of a young new leader."

"I can handle them." She gave him a soft smile, hiding the madness starting to build behind her icy eyes.

He pulled her into a quick hug, sending Marlena into fight or flight mode. "Stop being fucking weird. Hug me back." His laugh rumbled against her.

She wrapped her arms around him quickly, giving his back a few awkward pats. Marlena forced him to let her go as she brushed through the ends of her hair that had been squished between their bodies. "You're messing my hair up." Marlena swatted at him, taking a step back so she was no longer within his reach.

He chuckled. "See you tomorrow?"

They were all supposed to get together for early morning training with Bridger before leaving Fortis. "Yeah, tomorrow."

Marlena watched him walk away, dropping her mask when he was gone. Her shoulders rolled back, and that playful, sweet demeanor fell.

*I'm going to need to keep an eye on him.*

Ivelle opened the door after Marlena's first knock. She stepped to the side immediately, letting her in.

"What happened?" she asked, closing the door and locking it.

Marlena met her eyes with a serious expression. "I have your first task."

Ivelle smiled, her eyes lighting up. *Eager to serve.*

"I need you to distract Khort. He has too much free time on his hands. He doesn't need to be left wandering the halls after meetings when most of the time, I have to sneak away after them to chat with our allies." Marlena sat on the end of Ivelle's bed.

Ivelle gave her a fake innocent smirk. "And how would you like me to distract him?"

Marlena snickered, genuinely finding the excitement in Ivelle's tone amusing. "However you'd like." She winked. "I've heard shifters are animals in bed."

Ivelle rubbed her hands together, licking her lips. "Keep your friends close and your enemies closer."

*But Khort is your friend.*

Many have felt the gods' presence. It's not unheard of that they make themselves known, but there's never been a firsthand account of what they say if they were to answer back. Anyone who's gotten that close has never lived to tell the tale.

## Twenty-One Years Old

"Whatever is going on between the two of you, figure it out. Get in the ring." Bridger pointed to the middle of the room, where a circular one-on-one fighting mat sat.

Marlena and Ivelle didn't even have time to walk across the room before Vega rolled her eyes at her sister's presence.

It'd been over a week since their fight in Vega's bedroom, and they hadn't hashed out their disagreement about Vega's life and how Bridger fit into it. In fact, they had barely talked.

Meaning, Marlena hadn't been able to see Arlet either. She was busy. The months leading up to the transition of a Curia seat were exhausting. Even if Marlena weren't also planning on overthrowing the current government, she would've been busy.

Every waking moment was either pretending to be fine or plotting her parents' demise. There weren't many hours left in the day afterward to do much with.

Arlet sat on a bench beside Khort, watching Marlena with intent.

Marlena scoffed. "I have no problem with her. Vega is the one acting like a child."

Vega's jaw dropped, but before she could storm forward, Bridger put his arm out in front of her. "No, we aren't doing this. You want to train? We train. And if you need to beat the shit out of each other to do so, I'll take it. In the ring. Now."

Bridger Dimico was going to be a hell of a commander one day.

Marlena raised a brow, nodding towards the mat with a cocky smirk.

Vega stared at her with a look she'd never seen before. Of course they bickered growing up, but nothing usually lasted more than a night. Whatever Vega was harboring this time still hadn't had the time to flicker out.

Vega let out a huff and leaned through the ropes, centering herself in the middle of the ring. Out of the whole group, Vega was the one most trained in hand-to-hand combat. And she should be, seeing as though she'd been fucking the commander's son for a year.

Marlena could hold her own though. She'd taken the training they'd been doing the most seriously... because she knew when and how it would come in handy.

Marlena unsheathed the two daggers at her thigh and let them clatter on the table Arlet and Khort sat near.

"Don't think you'll need those, huh?" Vega asked, her tone cheeky.

Marlena stepped into the ring, leaning her head against both sides of her shoulders. The joints around her neck popped, loosening up the muscles. "I don't plan on stabbing you in the heart, so no, I don't think they're necessary for me to win this match."

Vega kept her daggers in place as Bridger began to talk again. "You know the rules. No powers in the ring. Don't make me intervene." He climbed the side, positioning himself high enough where he could see clearly, and he started counting down. Before he got to one, the sisters had already circled around the mat, their eyes locked in a death stare.

Marlena raked her thumb over her fingers, popping her knuckles one by one, and waited for her sister to make the first move. She had to be on defense when in the ring with her, had to watch her every move.

Vega had been training with the greatest warrior Tolevarre had ever seen... and her new battle skills proved it. She faked a jump forward, causing Marlena to flinch. Her reaction made Vega laugh. Marlena's blood boiled, threatening to spill over and scorch everything it touched.

*She's mad at me for telling her the truth. If she only fucking knew...*

Marlena didn't wait for Vega to lunge again, deciding to take a page out of Vega's own book. *Strike first. Don't give them the chance to outsmart you before the fight even begins.*

As if Vega was ready for it, she dodged Marlena with ease and used the forward momentum Marlena had been riding to trip her up. Marlena fell to the mat with a thud that echoed through the room.

"Nice!" Khort pounded on something from behind, leading in the hooting and hollering of the crowd starting to form around them. It was early morning, and soldiers were starting to trickle in for their training sessions.

Marlena hopped up quickly, not giving Vega enough time to land another blow. She clenched her teeth, realizing she had to get inside Vega's head. It was the only way she could stop her from focusing on every single move she made. "Is that all you've got?"

Vega grumbled. "Shall I remind you how many times you've lost to me during a sparring session? Or do you not want people to know that the future leader of Amora can't fight her way out of a corner?"

"Ooooohhhh," people around the ring sang in unison, a few snickers mixed in.

Marlena barked a laugh. "Don't get too cocky, sweet sister. It's not a good look on you." She blocked Vega's next move, landing a blow to her face with the tip of her elbow.

Blood ran down Vega's nose. She wiped it away with the palm of her hand, smearing red across her cheek while it continued to trickle to the mat underneath their feet. "Says the cockiest woman I know."

It was working. Marlena was getting under her skin, which meant she would start to lose focus—it was Vega's biggest weakness on the mat. Bridger had pointed it out a few weeks ago, and Marlena was using that to her advantage.

"I like to call it confidence." Marlena leapt forward with a jab to Vega's side. She hunched over, giving Marlena just enough time to swipe her leg under her feet and bring her to the ground.

Vega moved with a quickness Marlena hadn't been expecting, twisting herself on top of her, forearm pressing against her collarbone. "Oh yeah? Who's confident now?" she jeered, moving her hands to hold Marlena by her wrists.

Marlena bucked her hips, but Vega held strong, pinning her down in all the places she should be able to use to overpower her. Marlena was bigger than Vega, in height and weight, but Vega was smart... knew what to do to have the advantage in a fight.

Marlena screeched with anger, annoyed she'd let her sister pin her. But she wouldn't lose; she couldn't.

She threw her head forward, skull cracking against Vega's. Stars exploded in her vision, but when Vega's grip loosened, Marlena fought against the pain in her head. She wrapped one of her legs that had been pinned under Vega's knees around her, using her weight to flip positions. Marlena held her down, using one of the missing daggers she'd snuck from Vega's sheath.

Marlena pressed it against her throat, signaling the end of the match... but she wasn't done. "You can't be mad at me forever," she spat.

Vega writhed underneath Marlena, never willing to give up a fight easily. "I'm not mad, Marlena!" she screamed. "I'm sad! I'm sad that you think what everyone else is saying is true!"

The room quieted, and Marlena unintentionally loosened her hold on Vega. "Vega, I—"

Vega didn't let her finish, flipping out from underneath her to stand. Marlena stayed crouched on the floor, looking up at the tears welling in Vega's eyes. "Shut up, just shut up!" She stomped her foot like they were children again. "You can't rule my life! You can't tell me how I'm supposed to feel, how I'm supposed to react. This is my life, *my life!* Not yours." Vega fought her tears, wiping at the blood drying on her face.

Marlena stood slowly, and Vega snatched her dagger from her hand, returning it to the holster on her leg. "I just want to protect you, that's all."

"You can't protect me from everything. I don't want you to." Vega's words were soft, only loud enough for those who were closest to the ring to hear. "I want to live my own life, make my own decisions, get hurt if that's what's going to happen. If Bridger breaks my fucking heart, all you need to do is be there for me. Be my sister..."

Marlena bit the inside of her cheek so hard she could taste the metallic tang of blood. "The world is changing..." She looked over her shoulder, noticing the number of eyes on them. She took a step forward. "And I want you to be a part of the change. I don't want you to get left behind, Vega."

Vega squared her shoulders, blinking away any remnants of the sadness that had lingered in her gaze. "Have you ever thought about what I want? That maybe I just want to be left alone?" And before Marlena could respond, Vega stormed off and left her by herself in the middle of the ring.

A victor, and yet she didn't feel like she'd won.

Bridger cleared his throat the same time the training room door slammed shut. "Marlena wins."

Marlena scanned the room, eyes connecting with everyone who

stared. Some lingered, but others scurried away before she could scare them off with the anger sizzling behind her cold eyes.

When Marlena's gaze fell on Arlet, her stomach turned.

*I won't make it out with the people I thought I would... Strike first.*

## TWENTY-TWO YEARS OLD

*My birthday. The year I take over the Amora seat. The year I overthrow a thousand-year-old government.*

One month... That was all that separated her from the beginning of the end.

Marlena's eyes popped open, and the seconds turned to minutes as she lay there staring at the ceiling. Twenty-two years old, and she was still waking up alone in her large bed big enough for four grown adults.

Inhaling slowly, she sat up, taking in the bright morning light starting to peek through her curtains. The sun hadn't fully risen yet, but the white snow littering Amora year-round always made things brighter.

Marlena stretched her arms over her head, and as she got out of her bed, a little gust of her wind opened the curtains to let the sunshine in. It wasn't often the sun peeked through the clouds this time of year. Marlena wouldn't waste a minute of it.

It took her eyes a few seconds to adjust to the new lighting, but when they did, Marlena stood by her window, staring blankly until a tap on the door saved her from the racing thoughts inside her head.

Ivelle peeked in. "Morning." Marlena nodded, inviting her in without a word. Ivelle strode over to Marlena with a cup of tea in her hands, a small and genuine smile making her already gorgeous face shine. "Happy birthday."

Marlena looked at her cousin, unsure of the emotion welling in her chest as she reached out and grabbed the tea Ivelle offered. Steam rose from the fresh beverage, the smell of peppermint and honey waking Marlena fully.

*Honey.* Marlena's thoughts instantly clouded with images of Arlet. She brought it to her lips and rested it there as she closed her eyes and took a deep breath, trying not to lose herself in the scent.

When she opened her eyes, there was a tiny smile on her own lips. "Thank you."

Ivelle glowed at Marlena's admiration.

Marlena tipped the cup, finally taking a sip of the tea. Ivelle had made it perfectly. "Either you've been paying attention, or you're taking credit for the help's work."

Ivelle winked, picking the hem of her white dress off the floor as she sat in the lounge chair by the simmering coals of last night's fire. "I'll never tell."

The two had slowly begun opening up about their childhoods, learning their mothers had similar techniques when it came to raising daughters. Celeste wasn't quite as harsh as Ryanna, but Ivelle's mental scars were still prominent.

They talked until a guard came to announce a visitor. Marlena glanced down at her knee-length nightdress. "Who is it?" she asked the guard, whose eyes never wandered from hers, despite the lack of clothing Marlena wore. When she stood, she watched the muscles in his face tense as he fought to remain professional.

"I told him it wasn't really necessary that he announce my arrival." Arlet's voice got louder as she snuck around the guard in the doorway, ducking under his arm holding the door open. Arlet entered with a neatly wrapped box, clearly aggravated by whatever had happened before coming in. "We went to school together for ten years, Poe. I'm not here to assassinate her."

The guard hadn't looked familiar to Marlena at all… *Oops*.

"I take my job very seriously." His gaze returned to Marlena, waiting.

She shooed him away.

Ivelle stood, taking Marlena's empty mug from the table. Marlena hadn't told her much about Arlet, but Ivelle had asked multiple times what the plan was with her… How long would Marlena keep her in the dark? "I'll give you two some privacy." She said a quiet hello to Arlet and closed the door behind her.

Arlet took a deep breath, and Marlena watched the tension free from her shoulders. "I've been outside arguing with him for fifteen minutes." She wandered over to the dying fire, spinning in circles to warm herself. She was always cold, and this hellish territory didn't help with that.

Marlena watched her curiously, eyes fixed on the box. "Why didn't you just come in?"

Arlet stopped, catching Marlena's gaze over her shoulder. "Because I didn't want to get stabbed or bit by a bear. Poe's a really, really large bear in his shifter form."

"He wouldn't have lived to see another day if he had laid a single finger on you." Marlena's eyes wandered to her ass, a lazy smile on her lips when she made her way back to Arlet's eyes.

Arlet rolled hers. Marlena knew she didn't believe her, but she should. Marlena would rip Poe's arms off and make the others—

"What are you thinking about?" Arlet asked.

Marlena zoned back in, the thoughts about dismembering her guard pushed to the back of her mind. "My present," she answered, covering for the sinister thoughts she'd interrupted.

"Oh gods, yes, Mar." Arlet crossed the room, passing the box to her before pressing a light kiss on her cheek. "Happy birthday."

Marlena held the box in her palms, looking down at it. Vega, Arlet, and Khort had always bought her a joint present growing up, so when Marlena looked at the little tag hanging off the emerald ribbon and found only Arlet's name on it in her pretty handwriting, a warmness spread through her chest.

Love. She knew it before it fully clicked. Marlena loved Arlet. She'd always had love for her, as her sister's best friend—as *her friend.*

But this feeling was new, and one she hadn't felt before.

Arlet stood with one hand clasping the opposite elbow. "I thought maybe you could wear it tonight for your birthday dinner."

Marlena opened the box, setting the lid to the side. Staring back at her was the most gorgeous emerald gown folded neatly inside. Marlena's lips parted as she ran her free hand over the silky material.

Arlet stepped up and put each hand on either side of the box and held it in place, allowing Marlena to grab the dress by its corset top and hold it out in front of her. The straps fell to the side, hinting to a little off-the-shoulder number. The dress was sleek, form-fitting, and the perfect cut for Marlena's body.

When Marlena looked from the dress, catching Arlet's gaze again, Arlet was biting the inside of her lip nervously. "I saw it on a mannequin in Demuto last week and knew you had to have it."

Marlena laid the dress to the side carefully. She grabbed Arlet gently by the cheeks, her thumb grazing over the spot she was still gnawing at from the inside. "What's wrong? You're not worried I hate the dress, are you?" Marlena asked. "Because I love it."

Arlet shook her head and stopped fidgeting to take a deep breath. "You haven't—you never reached out after Ivelle found us. I started to wonder if you maybe thought this wasn't worth the risk anymore..." She had always been the more reserved of the group— the one who felt out of place around them. Marlena, the future leader. Vega, the storm-wielder. Khort, the dragon. Bridger, Tolevarre's strongest warrior.

On late nights when it was just the two of them, Arlet had opened up about her secret quandaries. She didn't feel strong enough. How would she ever rule over a territory, one that had given up on her years ago, with nothing to offer it?

*Vates is a lost cause, but Arlet isn't.*

"Arlet," Marlena said on a breath, running her thumb over her full lips. "I didn't intend on making you feel that way... I'm just busy. There's a lot going on behind the scenes and—" This wasn't the time to tell her. "I want you. I didn't want to leave you that night, but I had to make sure that if we tell people about us... *when* we tell people about us, it's us who get to make that decision. Not Ivelle."

Arlet wrapped her arms around Marlena's torso. "You two look like you're getting along," she commented.

Marlena pushed a stray curl out of Arlet's face. "She's coming around."

Arlet's face lit up with a smile. "Good. I—"

Marlena dropped one hand to rest on the small of her back, bringing their bodies together and disrupting Arlet's thoughts. "You?" She raised a brow but knew the look in her eyes was enough to get her off the topic of Ivelle.

The worry washed off Arlet's face as she leaned in for a soft kiss. "I'm glad you like the dress, and I know you're going to look magnificent in it, but I'm already planning on how I want to take it off you."

Chills ran down Marlena's spine as Arlet kissed down her jaw, suckling on the delicate skin of her neck.

"And all the ways I'm going to get you to moan my name tonight." Arlet's breath was hot on Marlena's skin. "How special I'm going to make you feel on your birthday."

It had been weeks since they'd seen each other, and over a month had gone by since they'd been caught in the hall with Ivelle. Since their little tryst began, the two hadn't been apart that long.

Time felt like it was speeding up, and Marlena still had no plan as to how she was supposed to tell Arlet what was to come.

*One more night... I can have one more night.* It felt like she counted in *one more nights* a lot lately.

"Since it's my birthday, can I request a preview?"

Arlet slid the nightgown straps down Marlena's shoulders, and it fell to the floor, leaving her completely bare and exposed to Arlet's sweeping gaze. "I suppose," she purred. This time, when Arlet bit her lip, it was with lust clouding her hazel eyes, not trepidation.

Arlet wasted no time grabbing Marlena's full breasts in her hands, twisting one nipple in her fingers and taking the other between her teeth with a light nip. Her tongue swirled around the bud until it was at its peak.

Marlena tangled a hand in Arlet's hair, a soft moan escaping her lips as Arlet continued the exploration of her body.

Arlet's gaze shifted from Marlena's chest to her eyes as she kissed her way back up to her mouth. "I've missed you so much," she mumbled against her skin.

Arlet backed her up until she bumped into the loveseat. Marlena sat, watching Arlet fixate on the warmth she knew was waiting for her between Marlena's thighs.

Being the center of attention sent Marlena into a lustful spiral, the feeling of being wanted pulling her down into a sea of need. She positioned herself on the armrest of the couch and spread herself wide, sliding her fingers through the slick lips of her pussy. "Did you miss how wet she gets for you, pet? How hot I get when I think of your mouth on me?"

Arlet sank between her legs, answering Marlena's question by dragging her tongue between her slit. She hummed in response to Marlena's hips bucking.

Marlena gripped the back of the couch. Arlet continued to work her tongue against Marlena's clit, switching between flicking and sucking in perfect synchrony.

"Oh my gods, yes," Marlena cried softly, locking eyes with Arlet at the same time she slid two fingers inside her. "Such a good girl. You know exactly how I like it."

Arlet expertly pressed into Marlena's soft spot, then pulled her fingers all the way out, only to plunge them back in with more power each time.

Marlena let one hand slide up her body, massaging her nipples for more stimulation.

"That's it. Play with those perfect tits while I make you come." Arlet removed her mouth from Marlena's clit, replacing it with her thumb. "Fuck, Marlena. You're so hot."

The groan escaping Arlet's mouth flipped a switch inside Marlena. She stopped touching herself, yanking Arlet up by her underarm, and captured her mouth with hers. Marlena didn't have to wait for Arlet to open her mouth—she'd eagerly opened it the second their lips met.

Marlena sucked Arlet's tongue into her mouth, tasting herself, causing another wave of pleasure to rack through her while Arlet continued to use her fingers to bring her to the edge of an orgasm.

Her walls tightened, gripping Arlet's fingers as she neared her climax. Marlena whimpered, losing sight of the person she was supposed to present herself as.

Arlet pulled away from her lips and kissed down her body until she was back between her legs. She sucked the inside of Marlena's thighs, surely leaving marks, her eyes staying fixed on Marlena's core while pumping her fingers in and out. "That's it. Let me hear you." Her tongue met her now overly sensitive bud, and within seconds Marlena's body shuddered.

Her head flew back, her long blonde hair cascading down her spine, and she moaned Arlet's name loud enough for the whole home to hear.

Arlet lapped up the cum spilling out of Marlena and cleaned her fingers with her tongue. "Sweeter than any cake I'll eat tonight."

Gods, Arlet was a different woman when it was just the two of them—so sure of herself, so strong. Marlena could see the woman she could become with a little coaxing and praise.

Gone was the girl who was timid and unsure of herself, and in her place was this minx of a woman, ready to wreak havoc on Marlena's body and mind.

"Fuck, come here." Marlena pulled Arlet back up to her lips, devouring her like she could be the one to rid Marlena of all the wrongdoings in her life.

*If I had fallen for Arlet sooner, could she have been able to save me?*

"Mom and Dad had to go to Pax for something last minute, and they won't make it back. They said to give you a hug from them." Vega pulled Marlena into a tight squeeze, one her parents had never, *and would never,* give her. "Happy birthday," Vega said, showing no sign of resentment from their recent fight.

It was custom for their family to get together with their closest friends for every birthday, and while she didn't particularly care if her parents were here or not, it just went to show how little she meant to them—even after all this time, after all the work she'd done to be exactly what they'd wanted her to be.

They would be celebrating Saturnalia next week, officially marking two weeks until Marlena was to take over Amora.

Two weeks until Marlena stabbed her parents in the back and took everything they'd ever loved from them.

The details were in place. Everyone knew when and where to attack. They all knew their jobs and the roles they would play... It was Marlena who had started to question herself.

How would she tell her sister? How would she convince Arlet

what she was doing would be better for their world in the end? Would they be better off not knowing until the job was done? What if Marlena wasn't strong enough, hadn't planned everything well enough?

*What if I am the incompetent fool my parents think?*

"Marlena."

Her head jerked from the spot she'd been staring through the floor.

"You good?" Vega asked with her eyebrows scrunched together.

"Mm-hmm. Yes, of course. I just..." Marlena bit her lip. "Remember when we went to Littera and got those books about summoning gods?"

Vega blew a laugh from her nose. "Yeah, I think I still have one tucked under my bed somewhere." Her smile faded a bit. "I can't believe we ever even entertained the idea of doing something like that. It's a fucking suicide mission."

And that was the end of that conversation. *For now.*

Vega nodded towards the dining room where everyone had been called for dinner. "C'mon, let's go celebrate the twenty-two-year-old you, the almost-leader of Amora."

Dinner went by without a hitch. Khort's parents had shown up, gifting Marlena a sweet snowflake necklace she would never fucking wear.

Ivelle and Khort disappeared sometime before dessert was served after making eyes at each other all night. Ivelle had been keeping Khort expertly preoccupied, so much so, Marlena wondered if her feelings were starting to become genuine.

Arlet and Vega lounged in the sitting room with Bridger, who poured everyone a glass of wine, offering one to Marlena when she walked in.

Her mind raced with thoughts tonight, and no matter how many glasses she put down, Marlena couldn't get them to stop. The voice in her head was looming in the back too, waiting to strike when her walls were down. "I think I'm going to go to bed. I'm supposed to have a meeting in the morning with our parents. Best I be bright and chipper for that."

Arlet narrowed her eyes, catching the shift in Marlena's mood.

Vega groaned. "You're no fun anymore. What happened to you?" It was a joke, but Marlena winced slightly at the question.

"I've never been as fun as you, dear sister. I was raised to rule, not throw lavish parties." Marlena leaned between Arlet and Vega, popping a kiss to her sister's cheek. "Thanks for tonight."

Marlena ran a friendly hand over Arlet's shoulder, ignoring the heat of their touch. "Goodnight." She nodded a goodbye to Bridger, who watched her with dark eyes. "Make sure these two drink some water before bed, okay?"

She didn't wait to hear if he responded before walking up the stairs on silent feet. Marlena slipped into one of the many guest suites in the west wing of the Aeris home, and without taking her dress off, she fell into bed and curled up under the plush covers.

Something had hit her tonight, a feeling she wasn't sure she could find a name for. But her mind kept wandering to all she had planned and of all she might lose if she went through with it.

That little voice woke up, reminding her of everything she didn't have.

*Your parents don't love you.*

*Your sister will never choose you when this all goes up in flames.*

*The woman you're in love with will never be who you want her to be.*

*No one trusts you.*

The door to her room opened, letting in a stream of light before it disappeared. The pitter-patter of Arlet's footsteps took up space in the quiet room, even though it was obvious she was trying to be silent as she slipped out of her shoes and crawled into bed next to Marlena.

"You're still in your dress? Were you hoping I'd get the hint and hurry up to help you take it off like I promised?" Marlena could picture the sultry look in Arlet's eyes.

Arlet's hands wandered up the curve of Marlena's body, but for the first time since they'd started sleeping together, Marlena grabbed her hand and hugged it against her chest. "Will you just lie with me?"

Arlet went still. "Mar, what's wrong?" She rested her chin on Marlena's shoulder from behind.

For a second, Marlena let her walls come down. "What if I can't do it? What if I'm not strong enough?"

"You were born to do this." Arlet answered without knowing exactly what it was Marlena was talking about, nuzzling against her cheek. "I believe in you. I always have."

*If only she really knew who you are at your core.*

"I don't want to do this alone," Marlena whispered.

"You don't have to. I'm here." Arlet pulled her arm from against Marlena's chest and started to smooth the soft hair on her scalp.

Marlena closed her eyes, letting herself fall into Arlet's sweet touch. "I want to tell people about us." If they let people know they were together, then maybe Marlena could come clean about her plan. *One step at a time.*

There was silence for longer than Marlena hoped for when laying her heart on the line.

"We should wait until after you're sworn in. I don't..." There was a pause. All that could be heard was their soft breaths. "I don't want to mess anything up for you. If your parents aren't happy with your choice, they could take this from you."

"They love you. You're like a second daughter to them." Marlena rolled over, her nose bumping Arlet's.

"Third. A third daughter," Arlet corrected, but Marlena didn't have the energy to explain that she'd never been a daughter to her parents—she'd always been a means to power.

Marlena could see the faint lines of her face this close, her eyes adjusting to the soft moonlight popping through the curtains. "You're a future leader too." She knew Arlet was right... Her parents would never approve, not when Arlet had nothing to offer. No powers, no territory.

"A future leader of what?" Arlet uttered a sad laugh. "Vates is gone... and so are its people." Arlet brushed her hand over Marlena's cheek. "And I'm as powerless as I've ever been." Sadness laced her tone so deeply, Marlena felt it in her own chest. "Let's just wait, okay? Let you settle into your role, and then we can talk about this again one day. For now, let's just keep doing this. More of this."

Marlena's throat tightened. "And what is this?"

"I..." Arlet went quiet again, nibbling on her lip. "I don't know, but we have plenty of time to figure it out." She placed a kiss on Marlena's lips, one unlike any of the others. "Get some sleep. We can talk about this again soon, okay?"

Marlena nodded, unsure of what else she could say.

*What if I don't need the dead gods to rule? What if I need them to fix what's broken inside me?*

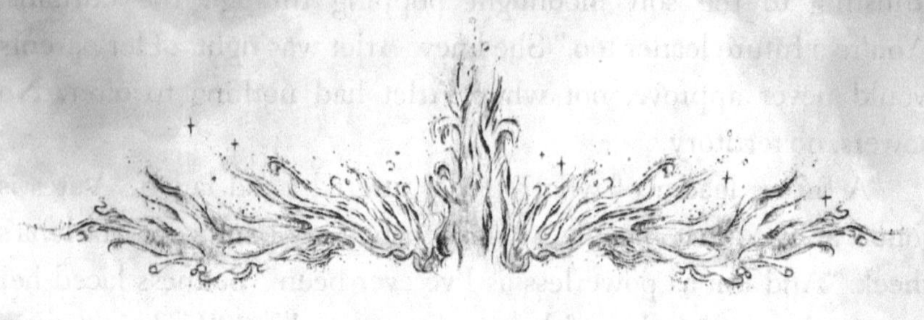

## Twenty-Two Years Old

Marlena woke to an empty bed... again.

After last night's conversation with Arlet, she was on edge. So the second her mother sighed heavily about Ivelle joining them for the meeting this morning, Marlena's anger rose, and she had nothing left in her to hide it. "You know, Mother, you once told me that sighing too often was a sign of emotional incompetence." She and Ivelle took a seat at the end of the table, across from her parents.

"Oh, so you do listen when I speak. Fascinating." Ryanna rested her hands on top of the table. "Which means you heard me when I told you that you wouldn't be granted Ivelle as your second in charge."

Jonan sat quietly, as he usually did when his wife was going rounds with his eldest daughter.

"With all due respect, you don't get to pick who Marlena's second is. Her choice is implemented after she's sworn in, which means you then have no control over Amora or what happens there." Ivelle's attitude had changed since Marlena promised her what she wanted—power—but the fierceness behind Ivelle's eyes had always been there... and now it was clearer than ever. "And you're the ones who wanted me to learn from Marlena in the first place."

Marlena and Ivelle weren't friends, but they were on mutual ground. Ivelle knew she'd never get anywhere without Marlena paving the way, and Marlena knew it would be easier to have someone around to do her dirty work.

"Ivelle, shut up." Jonan spoke, finally interjecting in the women's spat.

Marlena glared at her father, nails digging into the oak table. "No, we're not doing that. I am two weeks away from ruling part of our realm, and I can make it very easy or very hard for the both of you."

Ryanna scoffed at her. "Ruling? We've told you this before. You don't get full control. We still have an agenda we plan on keeping. We think it's just time for a new face in the public eye. If we got nothing else right with you, at least you're beautiful... someone people are willing to follow blindly." But we can still call this whole thing off. If we say we think you're not fit to run Amora, we can leave it up to a vote again."

*All you are is a pretty face.*

"Shut the fuck up," Marlena responded to the voice in her head. When she realized she said the words out loud, she moved on as quickly as she could to distract Ryanna from staring too intently. If she stared hard enough, would she see through Marlena's facade? "How well did that go for you the last time? I think a lot has changed since I was sixteen... I think a lot of people see something else in me that wasn't there then." Her icy gaze held her mother's. Marlena wasn't that girl anymore.

*I'm worse.*

"And what does Arlet think?" Jonan asked, snatching Marlena's attention.

For a millisecond, Marlena's mask fell, but she snapped it back into place as fast as she could. Unfortunately, it seemed her parents noticed the slip.

"I caught her leaving the room you stayed in very early this morning, still in the dress she wore last night." Ryanna tilted her head with a knowing sneer.

Marlena saw herself in her mother then, realizing she shared so many of her mannerisms. *Oh no.*

"And I thought that was a little strange, seeing as though she lives right down the hall and had every opportunity to go to her own room last night."

Jonan stretched his legs out under the table and put his hands behind his head. "When your mother told me, I questioned some of the help... and it seems you two have been spending a lot of time together."

"We've been friends since we were children. We've always spent a lot of time together," Marlena countered.

"Oh, Marlena. Please. There's no use in lying to us when it's so clear we know the truth." Ryanna had this smile on her lips that made Marlena's eye twitch—made her want to rip that smug ass look right off her fucking face.

"We have put up with a lot of things when it comes to you." Jonan sat up straight, his hands clasped on the table in front of him. He was the picture of ease, with his peppered dark brown hair brushed back in the perfect wind-tossed style he liked to wear it in. His white blouse was unbuttoned a few, bringing attention to his toned chest.

He didn't look like the type of person he was on the inside.

Rotten.

"But this little thing you've got going with Arlet stops now. We won't watch you waste your life away with someone who can offer you nothing in return. You should be holding out for when Bridger gets bored of Vega." Jonan leaned back in his chair again, relaxing like he'd already won the argument before it even started. "We're looking out for you. You should be grateful."

Talking about Vega was one thing, but their snarky attitudes were what made Marlena lose whatever patience she had left— which wasn't much. "Grateful?" Marlena spat, her chair scooting back as she stood. "You're trying to take yet another thing from me!"

Ryanna let out another long, drawn-out sigh. "Must you be so dramatic?"

"You think this is me being dramatic?" Marlena asked, her voice rising as she pointed at herself. "My whole life you've been taking from me. You took my childhood, pressing me to be ready for the Curia. Then you tell people I'm not powerful enough and try to snatch not one, but *two* seats right out from underneath me after abusing me for years."

Ivelle paled, hands gripping the arms of the chair like she was ready to spring from it at any second.

Jonan had begun to turn red, but Ryanna's anger spiked quicker. She jumped to her feet, leaning across the table at Marlena. "We didn't abuse you, Marlena. Don't you dare go around spreading lies."

Marlena's jaw dropped, completely unhinged from the shock. "You're fucking kidding me, right? You locked me in a room with no food and barely enough water to survive when I was *nine!* You caged me like a feral fucking animal and made me use the bathroom in a corner. You took every opportunity you had to remind me that I wasn't good enough, that I would never be good enough! And now you want to take the one person who's shown me that I'm worth loving? After everything you've done, you're willing to take more?"

Ryanna rolled her eyes, reeling with annoyance like Marlena was throwing a temper tantrum. "Get a grip! We loved you. Everything we did to you, for you, was out of love."

"You never loved me!" Marlena screeched, her breathing ragged. "You've never loved me!" She slammed her flat palms against the top of the desk, the sound of her rage echoing through the room.

Before Marlena saw it coming, her mother's palm connected with her cheek. "Don't you say that!" Ryanna hit Marlena so hard, her head snapped to the side and her ears rang.

Marlena cupped her face and rubbed until the sting wasn't as noticeable. The voice in her head, the one who was starting to sound a little too much like herself, roared to life. *Always the punching bag. When is enough, enough?*

Enough was now.

Marlena turned her head back to her mother, and a gust of wind swept Ryanna off her feet. The action took her back to the last time Marlena's mother swung on her. In this exact room...

With a swiftness not even Marlena knew she possessed, she caught her mother by the throat in midair before her feet made it back to the ground.

Ryanna hung suspended over her desk; Marlena's control of the wind assisted in keeping her mother dangling above.

Jonan jumped to his feet, making an attempt to throw himself over the desk at Marlena while Ivelle scampered backward. He never made it to his daughter. A stronger gust of wind split through Marlena's fingers, sending a desk flying. It took Jonan off his feet and pinned him to the wall.

Marlena stared into her mother's petrified eyes, squeezing on the sides of her neck until she started to turn purple.

She'd warned her not to touch her again.

Marlena pushed her cloak of invisibility over them both. She took a step back and slammed her mother down on the table like a human centerpiece.

The two of them couldn't be seen, and the wind circling the room drown out any noise Marlena might have made.

Marlena leaned down, close to Ryanna's ear, and loosened her grip to allow her mother a single, shallow breath. Marlena kept enough distance in between them to maintain eye contact. "That's the last time you ever lay a hand on me. I'm going to make you regret all of it. Him too."

Marlena dropped the blanket of invisibility and let her mother go before backing up a few steps. Her father spun in circles until his eyes landed on his wife, freeing himself from the desk only seconds earlier. Jonan dropped to his knees when he got to her, hands clutching Ryanna's cheeks while she heaved heavy breaths. Her neck was already bruising but would heal quickly enough with the ichor running through her veins.

Marlena only turned her back when her parents both set their stares on her, their faces mauled with a mixture of fear and fascination.

She didn't have to make sure Ivelle followed because she was already opening the door for Marlena. With her head held higher than ever before, Marlena stormed from the meeting room.

A guard heard the commotion and barreled down the hall at her. "Hey!" he called out, reaching for Marlena's arm.

*No one will ever touch me without my permission again.* Marlena spun around, catching him by surprise, and took him down without touching him.

He was a large man, and he didn't fall softly. The sound of his skull cracking against the floor should have made Marlena stop, but nothing could when she realized who this guard was.

The guard from outside the commander's office. The one from nearly four years ago who'd refused to give her the respect she deserved. What an unlucky time and place to be for him...

A slow and eerie smile crept across Marlena's lips when the guard's vision cleared and he, too, recognized the woman standing over him.

She wasn't the same young girl anymore.

Air-wielders could always feel the air around them. When their powers came to be, it could be hard to ignore what was once weightless. The strongest could feel the air inside objects... jars, water, anything with oxygen.

The air entering and exiting the guard's lungs was palpable to Marlena, taking up space in the room when she focused on his panicked breaths. He scooted back, trying to put space in between them—but every move he made away from her, Marlena took two steps forward.

This man couldn't run from his past.

He could get up and flee, and Marlena would still be able to feel his lungs contracting. She grabbed for the power within, snatching on to his air with a gentle first tug, watching as the guard gasped for the breath leaving his lungs.

One long draw, and Marlena drained his lungs of all oxygen. *And it wasn't even hard.* She stepped over him, lost inside herself while watching this man claw at his throat like it might help.

He was at her mercy... and Marlena wasn't letting go.

It was easy. *So easy.* To reach inside someone's lungs and cut off their air supply. Marlena had always wondered how simple it would be, but she'd never expected it was as effortless as taking a breath of her own.

She had always been too scared to try.

But not anymore. *I can't be scared anymore.*

Marlena was done being scared. Where had that gotten her?

The man's face started to turn blue, and his movements were becoming more erratic by the second. She imagined him begging for his life if he could.

*But he can't because you now have his life in your hands,* the voice inside said. Her voice. *My voice.*

"Marlena!" The scream was followed by a soft touch on her lower arm. *So featherlight. So soft.* So at odds with the fear distorting the usually ariose cadence.

It snapped her back into reality. Marlena let go of the air, and the guard inhaled a sharp, ragged breath, followed by gasps and coughs.

He was alive... but he had been so close to death.

Arlet stood beside her, both hands now on her arm with a bewildered look on her face. Her eyes were wide, and her chest rose rapidly with sharp, nervous breaths.

No one said anything.

Marlena looked around the room, taking in all the faces who'd witnessed her outburst. There was a mixture of shock, fear, and pain.

Even Ivelle stared like she hadn't known this version of Marlena had been hiding beneath her skin.

She'd been there all along... waiting.

Arlet's fingers felt like they were searing the skin from her bones. Marlena snatched her arm away, looking her dead in the eyes. "Do not touch me."

The look on Arlet's face would be one Marlena never forgot. But not even the hurt running rampant across Arlet's features could calm the piercing cold rage burning through Marlena's body.

*No one will stand in my way of getting the revenge I deserve.*

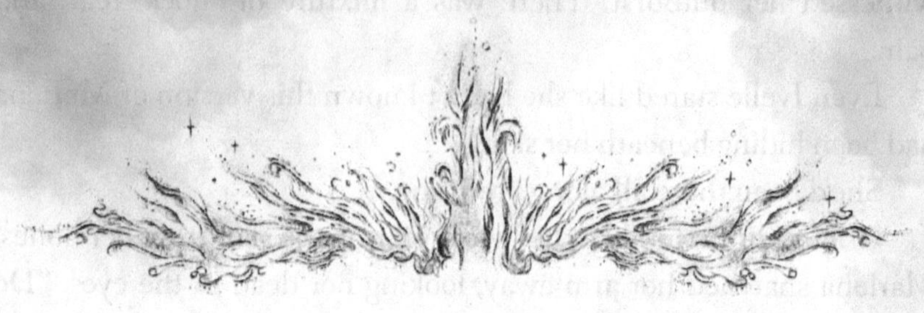

## Twenty-Two Years Old

One last Saturnalia.

Marlena caught a glimpse of herself in the mirror of the Aeris foyer as she and Ivelle made their entrance. Her long blonde hair was pulled up in a coronet braid, with random pieces falling down from her shorter front strands framing her face. The makeup she'd chosen was dark around her bright eyes, making them pop in contrast with the red stain on her lips.

Marlena's dress was unlike anything she'd ever worn before. The velvet was the color of fresh blood—*the blood that will soon splatter the halls of this home.* A single strap covered her shoulder, with another on the same arm falling around her bicep for decoration. The neckline cut low with tiny jewels sewn in, and the corset built in gave her a lift she was sure would get some attention. The fabric of the corset was see-through, giving a peep of the delicate skin underneath. The train of the dress spilled out behind her dramatically, her leg exposed from the slit running from the floor to her hip.

Long black lace gloves covered the skin of her arms, cutting off just above the elbow, and her shoes were high heels with thin black straps that wrapped up her bare leg—nothing that would take away from the dress itself.

Marlena left nothing to the imagination, allowing her figure to be the center of attention tonight.

*Distract.*

Marlena wasn't the same person she'd been last Saturnalia. She wasn't the same person she'd been a week ago.

Something inside her had changed in that room with her parents.

Their blatant disregard to the way they'd treated her was enough to change her mind on their fate.

They deserved worse than rotting in a cell for the rest of their miserable existences.

Heads turned as the two strode in from the cool night air.

Marlena hadn't spoken to her parents, Vega, Arlet... none of them since the incident with her mother. No one had reached out to her to make sure she was okay, and Marlena was sick of being the one to come back with her tail tucked between her legs.

*Never again.*

Arlet was the only one she felt a little remorse for, finding she really missed having her around—that she really, really wanted to tell her about what had happened and what was about to unfold.

But after much consideration, Marlena had decided to keep them out of it. They would follow when the time came. It was safer for them to be on the outside of this.

Marlena was going to make sure she made the entrance of a lifetime into the grand ballroom. *I will be remembered.* She stepped up to the door, and Ivelle fixed the train of her dress. She'd fallen in perfectly behind her, accepting that she was destined to follow—and Marlena was destined to lead.

Ivelle was right where Marlena wanted her.

The guard at the door nodded an amicable hello. The soldiers of Tolevarre would look at her differently now—they would respect and fear her after she'd nearly killed one of their own.

Marlena didn't return his hello; she only squared her shoulders and motioned for the double doors. They swooped open in a grand gesture, and a voice echoed over the crowd.

"Miss Marlena Caelum. Future Curia member of Amora."

"*And* Aeris," Ivelle added under her breath, allowing the announcer time to correct his mistake.

He did after a single sweep of Marlena's gaze.

Eyes of the entire room landed on Marlena. Hushed murmurs breaking out among the guests were heard even over the sound of the band's music.

A nobleman ascended the stairs, holding his arm out for Marlena to grab. She raked her gaze from his crooked elbow to his silver eyes. If it weren't for his dignity, Marlena was sure he'd be drooling.

She turned her head away from him and took the first step down the stairs by herself.

The last thing she needed was a man to step in where he didn't belong.

Once she reached the bottom of the stairs below, a servant with a tray of sparkling wine offered a glass to her. Marlena grabbed the stem between her fingers delicately and took a sip. As soon as the glass fell from her lips, her mother was at her side.

"Marlena, dear, you look lovely."

Marlena's eyebrows rose, a questioning look occupying her face as if to ask Ryanna, *What the fuck?*

Before she had the time to speak those exact words, her father popped in beside her. "We have been waiting for you." He eyed Ivelle taking her place behind Marlena's right shoulder. "There are a few people who'd like to meet the both of you."

Marlena and Ivelle shared a knowing look.

Had Marlena finally gotten her point across? *A shame.* It was too late for apologies.

The girls were swept away and into conversation by powerful families lucky enough to get an invite to her parents' famous Saturnalia ball.

It was clear where most of these people's alliances would stay when the time came, so she didn't bother remembering their names.

"Excuse me, I hate to interrupt, but I need to steal some of her attention for a moment." Vega's voice cut in before her hand slid into Marlena's, tugging her away from the group she'd gotten roped into talking about her plans for Amora with. Fake plans. Lies.

"Vega." Marlena tried to protest, but her little sister wasn't having it.

She yanked Marlena into a corner, turning around to finally look at her. "Where have you been?"

Shock ran through her body, the feeling of watching herself as an outsider rattling her enough to take a step back and look at Vega from the floor up like this moment wasn't real, like Vega was going to disappear before her eyes and this was all going to be a dream. "What?"

Vega's eyebrows scrunched together in confusion. "Mar, you attacked our parents, almost killed a guard, and then you went silent for an entire week. Now you're here, letting them parade you around like a proud show pony as if none of it happened."

Marlena didn't worry about hiding her eye roll. "'Attacked' is not the word you're looking for. I defended myself when our mother slapped me across the face. And that guard, well, he had that coming."

"She what?" Vega's eyes landed on their mother across the room, who averted her gaze from the two of them when she was caught staring. "What did you say that made her slap you?"

Marlena's teeth ground together so hard her cheeks vibrated. "What makes you think it was my fault?"

"Mom wouldn't—"

"I'm going to stop you." Marlena held her hand out. "This is one of those moments where you need to mind your business. What happens between Curia members, and what I do as punishment to a guard who deserved a reminder of who I am, is no matter to you. You don't get to insert yourself into anything you want anymore. You have to learn when to butt out."

Vega's jaw dropped, and her attitude that rivaled Marlena's growing rage spiked. "What is wrong with you? Why are you being so mean?"

"Mean?" Marlena wanted to raise her voice, to cause a scene, but this wasn't the time or place. Her allies were in the midst, mingling with the partygoers, putting feelers out for who might be useful at the turn of a new rule. Marlena took a breath, pinching the bridge of her nose. "Vega, stop worrying about things you can't control. About things that don't—"

"I'm worried about *you!* I don't care about the rest of it!" she screamed, cutting Marlena off.

*So much for not drawing attention.*

Marlena looked over her shoulder, noticing the eyes starting to flick to the two fighting sisters in the corner. She had to shut this down. Drawing a breath, Marlena looked back to Vega. "Oh, so now you've decided to worry about me? After nearly two decades, perfect little Vega has realized it's time to pay attention to what's going on behind closed doors?" Marlena had a slow smile spread across her lips. "It's too late for that. I need you to go back to what you were before. Clueless."

Vega would understand soon enough why Marlena was acting this way... why she needed to start pulling back and put some distance in between herself and the rest of their friends.

"Fuck you, Marlena." Tears welled in Vega's eyes, but she kept her head held high when she stormed away, not allowing Marlena to respond.

Marlena stared at the wall for a moment before she spun around and slid her pretty mask back into place.

She passed by a waiter with a tray and downed an entire glass of bubbly in a couple gulps, then put the flute back with a little too much force. The glass cracked, a spiderweb shatter traveling to its rim.

Ivelle spun on the dance floor with Khort, her laugh mixing with the sound of the music. She had taken her job very seriously—so seriously that he was still lost in their own world, a happy smile lighting up his handsome face as he and the most beautiful girl in their realm danced the night away.

Marlena silently hoped when this all fell down, Ivelle wouldn't rip his heart out. It seemed he might finally be able to let her sister go.

Crossing the room, Marlena was flagged down by a group of her parents' peers, and she would have gone to them if it weren't for the beauty in a bronze dress who caught her attention on the opposite side of the room.

Arlet's eyes twinkled against the lights strewn across the ceiling, but when they met Marlena's, she caught the sadness inside them and the dark circles underneath. Even with makeup, they were still visible in the shadows.

Marlena changed course, ignoring the group of brown-nosers. Her new path ended where Arlet stood. She held Marlena's stare until she was halfway to her, and she turned, leading Marlena away from the party. Her reaction didn't make Marlena stop... They were used to catching one another's eye across the room and sneaking off. It had been part of their game for months.

Marlena glanced over her shoulder every so often, ensuring no one was following or noticed them. Arlet snuck behind a door but left it propped open for Marlena.

The only sound in the library was the door closing with a click when Marlena shut it behind her. There were rows of shelves with books as old as the house itself, mixed Vin with newer collections.

Marlena had spent many nights studying here after the house went quiet and everyone else was asleep.

Arlet trailed down the middle row, her fingers skimming over books until she looked up and saw Marlena standing at the end and stopped.

"Hi," Marlena said with a smile pulling at the corners of her lips. *Gods, I've missed her*.

"Hi," Arlet squeaked back.

Marlena felt like she was floating as she walked down the aisle towards her. She reached out and grabbed Arlet's cheeks between her hands and kissed her softly. "You look fucking amazing," she mumbled against her lips.

Arlet didn't reach out and touch her like she normally would, and she didn't kiss her back with the need Marlena was used to.

Her hands fell from Arlet's face and traced the curves of her body, then rested on her hips. "Are you okay?"

Arlet immediately shook her head. "No."

The bags under her eyes were darker under the dim lighting between the shelves at night. Marlena fought the urge to bring her hand up and trace the lines of her face.

"Your parents..." Arlet started, biting at her quivering lip. "Your parents know about us. That's why you freaked out." It wasn't a question.

Marlena nodded, finally breaking the hold she had on her body and reaching up to push a piece of Arlet's hair behind her ear. Marlena was much softer with Arlet than she was with anyone else. This version of Marlena was fading, but with Arlet, she could save a small piece. For Arlet, she would.

"I didn't mean to get caught. I didn't mean to start all this trouble." Marlena could tell Arlet was doing her best to keep herself from crying.

She was hiding something. Marlena could feel it in the way her body stayed stiff, when she usually melted into her touch.

"It's okay. It's okay they know." Marlena traced a thumb over her cheek. "I told them I didn't care what they think, and I don't. They can't take you from me... I won't let them."

Arlet closed her eyes and leaned into Marlena's gentle touch. She kept her eyes closed when she spoke. "But I can." Her eyes popped open, and any trace of her sadness had been stored away, locked behind her hazel eyes.

Marlena's stomach dropped, and she stepped back. It could have been minutes, hours, or days before she finally spoke... and when she did, all she could manage was, "What?"

"But I can," she repeated. "I can take me from you."

The world seemed to spin on its axis, sending Marlena's stomach on a twisted ride. "What are you saying?"

Arlet seemed to be operating on autopilot, but her hands were shaking at her sides. She opened and closed her fists a few times, and they still shook with nerves. "Mar, I think..." She paused and swallowed, her throat bobbing. "I don't think we should do this anymore."

*No.*

Marlena had been pushing people away, scared in the end that they would give up on her but hoping they would see through the mask she'd been wearing—hoping they would see she was only doing this for now.

She could open up soon. *So soon.*

"No." Marlena's voice was quiet, her walls completely crumbling down around her like a war zone. *I can't lose her too.* She took a step forward, reaching for Arlet, but this time Arlet was the one to take a step back.

She shook her head, her jaw clenching as she fought against the tears. "I can't let you lose what you've worked so hard to get."

"I'm not. I won't." Marlena's heart felt like it was going to beat out of her chest. "Did they threaten you? Arlet, I swear to the gods if they—"

"No, they didn't threaten me. This isn't even about them knowing. It's about how you reacted, about how you treated Vega tonight, how you treated the guard... It's about you, Marlena." Arlet looked up at the ceiling, tilting her head back to avoid spilling tears. "Something is going on with you."

Even now, Marlena wasn't going to tell her what was coming. She couldn't use it as a last-ditch effort to keep Arlet. "I'm fine. I just have a lot going on."

"Of course you do, which is why you need to focus on yourself, on figuring out how to balance your new life and everything that comes with it. I can't be your distraction. I can't be the person you come to only when it's convenient to you, when you need to feel good."

"Do you think that's what I do? That I only come to you when it's convenient for me?" Marlena felt an emotion she hadn't ever felt before... one she never wanted to feel again.

*Heartbreak.*

"I think that's what it's turned into, yes. I know it's not intentional. I know you're busy, that your life is changing... but I—I only want what's best for you." Arlet's tears finally fell. She let them trail down her cheeks without wiping them away. "And I think what's best for you is something you don't want to confront yet... but us..." Arlet motioned between them. "This isn't good for you right now. You attacked your parents because they didn't want you to be with me, didn't you?"

"I didn't attack them because of you!" Marlena's anger soared, her wind rising with her emotions. Books from around the room clattered to the floor, and Arlet jumped in surprise. "I fought back! For the first time in my life, I showed them that I can't be messed with anymore!" Marlena hadn't realized she was crying too until she felt the moisture from her tears rolling down her neck. She wiped them away, smearing her makeup across her cheek. "Don't do this."

Arlet looked at her like Marlena was a stranger after taking in the mess she'd made of the library. *Just like Vega did...* "I don't have a choice," she choked.

"Yes, you do." Marlena couldn't find the strength to move. The power she'd felt in the ballroom earlier had dissipated, leaving in its place a version of Marlena she hadn't been since her childhood.

Sad.

Wounded.

*Weak.*

"I'm so sorry, Mar. I've loved every second of getting to see the person you are when no one's looking, and I want you to be that person all the time. I want everyone to see the person I've fallen in love with." Arlet's lips quivered. "But you can't be her until you're ready. Until you can trust that other people will love my version of you too."

Marlena tried to stop the tears, to patch her heart up before it shattered into a million jagged pieces... but it was too late. The dam broke, and there wasn't enough glue in the world to mend her broken heart.

"I love you." Arlet finally took a step towards Marlena. "But I can't fix what was already broken. I can't help you find yourself. Only you can do that."

*I love you.*

The words replayed in her head over and over again, turning frantic in the back of her mind. Marlena hadn't heard those words from anyone but Vega... and for the first time, they came from someone who didn't have to say them—who didn't feel obligated to love someone like her.

"Please don't leave me." Marlena's voice was barely audible even to herself, but somehow, Arlet still heard her.

She took another step forward and grabbed Marlena's face in her hands. "I will always be here for you. I promise. We just—we have to take a little break. You've gotta find out who it is you want to be, and the person you're being right now isn't the one I can be with." Arlet swiped her thumb over Marlena's face, catching a fallen tear. "I'm so sorry. Please don't hate me."

Marlena's hand covered Arlet's, the one that continued to wipe away the tears that wouldn't stop falling. She closed her eyes and memorized the way Arlet's hand felt against her skin.

"Say something. Please." Arlet's voice broke, the sorrow and regret in her tone magnifying the same emotions roaring inside Marlena's chest.

When Marlena's eyes snapped open, the tears had finally stopped. She pulled Arlet's hands away from her cheek and took a step back, wiping at her mess of a face before slamming her emotions behind the cold mask she'd been taught to wear.

"Marlena, plea—"

"Get out."

Arlet opened her mouth to say something, to plead with her, but Marlena had had enough. "Get. Out," she growled.

Arlet didn't move right away, and it almost looked like she was going to say something else, but Marlena couldn't let her.

She'd heard enough.

Her arm shot up, and with a gust of angry wind, the door to the library slammed open and cracked down the middle when it hit the wall behind it with too much force, pieces falling to the floor.

Arlet jumped again, the skirt of her dress fluttering with the movement. She nodded once and quickly took her exit.

Marlena watched her go, and when Arlet was out of sight and she could no longer hear her footsteps, Marlena fell to her knees and let out a shriek that might have shredded her vocal chords.

*Who are you now that no one's around to see?*

Even though no one knows what would happen if someone was successful in summoning one of the dead gods, one thing goes without saying: it might not be a world worth saving afterwards.

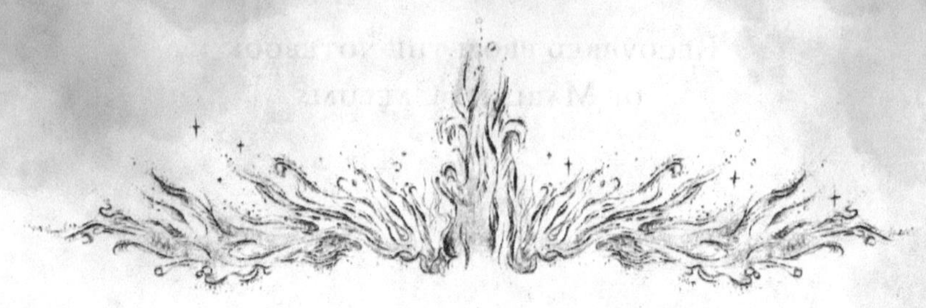

## Twenty-Two Years Old

The crowd below the balcony looked up, their eyes fixed on Marlena and her parents. All morning had been spent signing paperwork, turning over control of Amora to Marlena.

Only one thing stood between her and the start of a new life—the start of a new world. And that was being sworn in by the head priest and priestess of Oro, being presented to the people and the dead gods.

Her parents' hands were on her shoulders, one standing on each side. They'd both finished their speeches, her mother's drawing on longer than her father's. She wanted to thank all of Amora by name, it seemed, and then went on to boast about how she was excited to relax more... Oh, and "to hopefully plan a wedding!"

But now it was Marlena's turn to take the stage.

"People of Tolevarre, tonight, a new leader steps into place. Marlena Caelum." The oldest of the two acolytes, in stark-white robes, stepped forward. "It is time for you to take an oath with the old gods. Are you ready?"

Marlena nodded, taking a step forward with an exaggerated roll of her shoulders, forcing her parents' tight grips off. "I'm ready."

Not just for this seat... but for all of them.

"Please face the sky." Stella was as close as one could get to the stars in Tolevarre—as close as anyone could get to the dead gods.

Initiation ceremonies were always held in Stella, in the home she'd grown up in. It didn't matter what seat was being replaced, the leaders of Oro wouldn't allow them to happen anywhere else.

*"You need to be as close to the old gods as you can,"* they would always say.

Marlena's head fell back, and she closed her eyes.

"Marlena, all the dead gods are here with us tonight."

At his words, a rush of warmth swept over her entire body. Marlena could feel it, *feel them.* She'd attended only one of these her entire life, and while she was much younger, there was no way she'd ever forget this feeling.

*"Strong."*

*"What we need."*

*The gods are here.*

"They're here to guide you on your journey as a new leader, to watch the world their powers created live on."

The room was silent. All the attendees craned their necks up to the dark night sky with their eyes closed like everyone was praying in unison. People at home watched on their monitors, and if they didn't have one, they were at a local pub that did or were standing in their town squares, watching.

*Everyone will see what I've done. They'll know who's coming for them.*

"Repeat after me."

The priest began, and Marlena followed in his words. "I will guide my territory as if my ancestors and the original gods are with me. I am here to be a voice for the people, ready to put them first." No one ever meant those words. Marlena didn't feel bad for lying in front of the entire realm. "From now until my time is up, I will lead how the gods would have. I will be better than the last."

The prayer continued, Marlena reciting every word seamlessly. She'd known the acceptance prayer like a monologue since the age of ten. It had been beaten into her. A test she'd been forced to take countless times until she got it perfect.

"Marlena, open your eyes," the priestess said, taking a finger she'd dipped in a mixture of berries and red liquid to resemble blood and dragging it down the center of Marlena's eyebrows to her nose. "Marlena Caelum. Amora's newest leader."

*One down, eleven to go.*

Marlena swept away for pictures, but the smile she wore didn't reach her eyes. Eyes with a cold, blank darkness stared back in every photo.

Guards led Marlena to a back room, where she was allowed to wash the red stain from her face and get her makeup touched up before returning to the party.

But Marlena wouldn't be returning to the party right away.

Her reflection stared back at her in the bathroom mirror. A flash of the girl she'd been at nine distracted her.

Her eyes looked the same. Dead.

*Defeated.*

The dress she'd picked tonight had been intentional. A last goodbye to the girl she'd let steal her heart—to the only person who would ever break it.

When Arlet saw her in the green gown she'd bought Marlena for her birthday, it almost looked like she might break their unspoken no contact agreement.

But once she caught Marlena's glacial expression, she thought twice like a coward.

Marlena had known better. The voice in her head had warned her not to let Arlet get too close... and this was what she got for not listening.

It had never done her wrong.

And it wouldn't start now.

"Everyone get out." The staff and guards all looked at Marlena. Some might have had little question marks floating around their head if that were possible. "Did I fucking stutter?" she shouted.

Everyone scattered, leaving Marlena in the dressing room alone. She'd had a cloak stored inside the closet for her earlier, and the person who'd hidden it floated in.

"Is it time?" Ivelle asked.

Marlena grabbed the thick black cloak off the hanger and slipped it over her shoulders. "Is the horse ready?" she asked, ignoring her question.

"Yes. Your mare is waiting for you behind the garden like you asked." Ivelle leaned against the wall. "Marlena, what are you doing? Where are you going? We're supposed to attack tonight."

Marlena's wind whipped with her growing agitation. "Do you think I've forgotten about that?" Her laugh sounded foreign to her ears. "Everything I do, everything I've *done*, is for this night. Nothing has changed. I'm sealing our win." Marlena strode for the door, letting it open through a gust of silent wind. "Tell the others to wait. They'll know when it's time."

Slipping behind her invisibility, Marlena disappeared, sneaking out of the busy Aeris home and onto her horse without being seen.

Marlena pushed her horse to the brink of total exhaustion, not allowing her a break until they were deep in the patch of woods near a small and unpopular lake outside Stella. Her mare huffed, leading herself to water when Marlena left her unattended after dismounting.

Marlena emptied the bag she'd hidden in her cloak onto the forest floor. A box of matches, twelve candles, and the notebook she'd been hiding since her first trip to Littera fell from inside. Bringing it had been in case of emergencies. Marlena knew everything inside of it like the back of her hand.

Marlena grabbed the matches up and shoved them in her bodice, keeping them away from the snowy ground. Quickly, she placed the twelve candles in a circle around her.

One for each of the dead gods.

Mira had gotten it wrong.

Marlena wouldn't.

She'd spent too much time researching, too much time preparing.

Mira was careless. Marlena was careful.

With a match and a single breath, Marlena lit the twelve candles. Her control of the air from her exhale sent the flame in a perfect circle. The natural night air was calm, a few lone snowflakes falling from the sky.

Marlena sank to her knees, digging into the wet dirt under a small patch of snow, and opened her leather-bound notebook. She smeared the damp earth across the book, breaking into the very essence of the realm.

Her hands shook with nerves, but there was no time for that. There was no time to second-guess what she was doing.

She wouldn't lose.

Marlena wouldn't let herself become the person people expected. The girl who waited around for what she wanted.

*No. I'm going to get what I want. What I deserve.*

Marlena leaned her head back, and in a natural Latin tongue, she began to reach out to the gods who'd visited her once already tonight. "To the gods who were stolen from, who knew what our powers meant. To the gods who wanted more but had their lives cut short. I come to you tonight to promise liberation from the hell you've been trapped in. I come bearing myself as a vessel. I come to offer myself to you."

The wind around Marlena stirred, the flames of her candles breathing the oxygen swirling around her. Marlena's hair rose, and goosebumps formed on her arms.

"I feel you," she said, opening her eyes and looking around at the clearing and the foliage ruffling in the breeze. "No one has my rage. No one can promise you what I can. Mira was close, the closest anyone has ever been... but she wasn't right. She got it wrong. You don't care about love. You want power. Like me."

A candle's flame shot up, reaching out at Marlena. It didn't burn, but it seemed to watch her, examining her every move. She stared it down, watching the flame ride pieces of her wind.

But nothing more than a few elemental changes happened.

Marlena rose from the ground, turning to take in the circle. The sky was clouded with an oncoming winter storm, but above was clear, and stars twinkled in the darkness.

She could feel a presence slithering up her spine, but nothing spoke back. Nothing more than a few gusts of wind that weren't hers skirted above her head.

No one came.

And the longer she stood on the edge of the lake surrounded by pines, the warmer her body got from the rage of being ignored.

*You'll always be ignored.*

No, Marlena wouldn't be ignored, and she wouldn't fail. Marlena was the only choice the dead gods had.

Marlena was the only one who could promise them their own form of revenge.

"What is it you want?!" she screamed in the new language. "What must I prove to you?" Marlena spun, following a gust of wind with her eyes. "I am the one you've been waiting for. After thousands of years stuck in the in-between, you can finally let someone take over and get what you couldn't."

A bolt of searing heat poured through Marlena's body, burning every part of her until it settled in the core of her brain.

She stripped out of her cloak, the change in her body temperature becoming unbearable.

Lighter than a feather and softer than an early morning breeze, a voice inside her head asked the question she'd always wanted to hear —the exact one she'd asked them moments ago. *"What is it you want?"*

Marlena inhaled a sharp breath, but it caught in her chest when the voice rang again. *"Do not waste our time."*

She spoke out loud, unsure of how she was supposed to respond. "Power."

The voice changed this time, becoming something new. *"So does everyone else. What makes you so special?"*

"Because I want it the most."

A laugh tickled her insides, the sound lazy with a hint of pity. *"Everyone who's tried has wanted it, Marlena. You're no different."*

She stopped talking out loud, turning to the voice inside her head—leaning into the part of her who knew this was her destiny. *"Then why are you here? If I'm no different, you would have killed me already."*

No one responded, but Marlena could still feel the whispers. The voices mixed together like the hiss of an unintelligible argument. *"I am the first of our kind to have two powers. I'm not like the others."*

*"What about your sister?"* a new voice that was somehow different, yet still sounded like the others, clamored.

*"The sister,"* another voice hummed.

"She's not here!" Marlena screamed. She was so fucking sick of talking about Vega. "She's not here and she had the opportunity, but it's too late."

*"What makes you so sure you're the one for us?"* the first voice asked.

"Because I don't just want to rule. I want revenge. Revenge like all of you. I want the people who doubted me to suffer. The ones who made me question my worth... I want them dead. I want to watch the life drain from their eyes. I want to give you a body to call home again."

So many sighs of agreement rattled in Marlena's brain like a sweet caress.

Marlena knew she had them. It was the same feeling she'd had when Lucius joined her, when Ivelle fell in line. Like a fish to a worm... She just *knew*. "I'm not like Mira. Summoning you isn't just for me. It's for you. For us. Imagine the world we could rule if your powers became mine. I can get your revenge and mine too."

Marlena's skin burned with a fire she'd never felt.

*"And what are you willing to give us in return?"*

Marlena hesitated, and it wasn't nerves that kept her from answering right away. It was strategy. Her hook had sunk where it should, and now it was time to reel them in. "Anything."

The caress she'd felt inside intensified, as did the flames of her candles.

*"Anything?"* a new, louder voice hissed.

"Anything," Marlena confirmed.

Silence surrounded her at the same time the clearing went completely still. Her mare reared, braying in fear, and took off. Marlena could hear the twelve individual voices this time. *"Would you give us your heart?"*

Her heart.

Hearts.

Mira's still beating heart.

Before her nerves told her to run, Marlena shoved them down. Showing an ounce of weakness would get her killed. The gods didn't care about her... and she didn't care about them.

She wanted their powers, and she would lie however she needed to get them. Marlena wouldn't let them take over. She knew it was what they wanted—to make her body their host, erasing her own mind and taking over as they pleased. She'd told them she would be their vessel, but what they didn't know was Marlena would never stop fighting for the control she desired.

She'd lost too much already. She wouldn't let anyone else take more from her. Dead gods or not, Marlena would rule. This was her overtaking.

"What does my heart do for you?" she asked, watching the wind sweep around the treetops.

*"It shows us who you really are, who you're meant to be."*

Marlena's heart.

*My broken fucking heart.*

She'd lost everyone.

Vega wouldn't choose her.

Her parents had never loved her.

Bridger wanting anyone other than Vega was a complete pipe dream.

Khort would follow her sister anywhere.

And Arlet...

*Oh, Arlet.*

She had given up when Marlena needed someone the most.

What did Marlena need her useless heart for anyway?

"It's yours," she agreed, this time saying the words aloud again.

Power surged through her like the heat of Vulcan's flame, like the surge of Neptune's water, the strength of Mars's bones. All the dead gods rushed into Marlena one by one, taking up space that had once been only hers.

*"Show us your heart."*

*"Give it to us."*

*"You're ours."*

*"Such a wicked little thing."*

*"Rip it out."*

*You have nothing to lose.*

The last voice wasn't that of a god... it was the one she'd had in the back of her mind since before she could remember.

*"You must let go of it all, let go of every piece of yourself. That means ridding yourself of who you once were—of the people you once loved."*

The gods chimed as Marlena's hand rose to her chest, her manicured fingernails growing the claws of a beast. Pain blinded her, rushing through her body as her vision spotted, and she fought to stay in control.

The voices were loud. *So loud.*

A scream erupted from Marlena's throat, shredding her vocal chords until her voice sounded like that of an animal being devoured by its predator.

Her new claws pierced through the exposed skin on her chest, blood trickling down until it soaked into her dress.

"*Kill them.*"

"*They must die.*"

Marlena could barely hear the whisper of her own voice anymore, but before she plunged her hand into her chest, she could hear it saying, "They don't deserve to die."

It wasn't enough to make her stop. She couldn't stop.

The scream bubbling out of Marlena's chest must have rattled the entire realm, but she couldn't hear it through the pain ripping into her body, shredding through muscles and tendons, and breaking bones to wrap her fingers around her beating heart.

It pumped in her grasp, ticking in time with the pounding in her ears. Marlena took one last breath and pulled.

Her vision blurred, and blood splattered on the clean white snow... and in her hand, Marlena held the heart of a villain.

Marlena dropped to her knees, fighting to inhale a breath when everything went black. Her hands sank into the ground, and a green fire soared from her palms, melting the ground below. It consumed all it touched.

The wax of her candles didn't stand a chance and melted in the blink of an eye. Fallen pine needles lit, emerald sparks soaring in the growing wind to catch in nearby trees.

The embers of what Marlena's life had once been caught fire, spreading with a heat this world had never known. It didn't matter that the snow had saturated the greenery around her... Marlena's built-up anger set the forest ablaze.

Marlena's eyes snapped open, and she was thrust back into her body. A gasp of air reentered her lungs, and her gaze fixed on the flames pouring like lava from the palms of her hands.

The world around her shimmered with a new gleam—a power reborn.

The forest glowed, sputtering from her fire's heat. Marlena stood, and when she took a step, her body moved through time and space. Nothingness swallowed her whole, and when it spit her out, she stood behind her mother in the room where Marlena's story began.

She caught Ryanna's gaze in one of the mirrors, and reflected back to her was the face of a newborn woman. Her head dipped down, and Marlena's lips spread in a smile so eerie, she felt Ryanna's breath leave her lungs in a gasp of fear.

Claws shot out of Marlena's hand at her disposal, like a power that had always been inside her, and she caged Ryanna in like the prey she'd become.

And for the first time in her life, Marlena saw the world as she'd dreamed it to be.

*As mine.*

## THE END OF THE BEGINNING.

- PHYSICAL & MENTAL ABUSE
- TORTURE
- MENTIONS OF DEATH
- GORE
- MANIPULATION
- ABUSE FROM PARENTS
- THOUGHTS & PLANS OF MURDER

If there is a theme you are looking to avoid and it is not listed, or you think I should add one to this list, please reach out on my website and myself or someone from my team will respond as quickly as possible!

# Acknowledgments

My second book?! Wow! It wasn't any easier (thanks Marlena) but I think I've found my groove. Like I said last time, it truly takes a village to get my books from A to Z. Meet my village:

Josh, I couldn't have done this without your constant encouragement to follow my dreams and the acceptance that I will probably never have a normal life or schedule ever again. Thanks for reminding me that I can do this, even on the days I want to give up. I love you forever.

Mom, my forever number one fan. I wouldn't be the person I am without you. Thanks for raising me to stand up for myself and for the confidence to write badass women who don't take no for an answer!

Dad, thanks for raising a girl who can picture herself as the scary heroines in any book. I have definitely been called scary a couple times in my life.

Mollie, my soul sister. I wouldn't want to do this life without you. Thanks for being the yin to my yang, the Rachel to my Monica, the Glinda to my Elphaba—don't worry, I've forgiven you for not liking musicals. To many more years of hiding inside jokes in our books and requesting tables next to each other at every convention we attend. You are why I believe the found family trope is top tier.

Kristen, my social media manager, my playlist coordinator, the other half of my brain, part of the committee, and one of my very best friends. Thank you for being here with me, for letting me ramble about my ideas, and for sitting on FaceTime in silence for hours just to make sure we're getting work done. Hope you're ready to do this with me forever!

Bobbi, at this point, you have a permanent home in Tolevarre. Pick a territory and I'll make sure your home is safe from the dawning war. Thank you for reading Heart when it was a mess and then giving it those perfect Bobbi touches at the very end.

My SBP fam, for being there when I needed a night away from my fake world. Y'all really know how to keep a girl grounded.

My beta readers, A.M Wright., Haley C., Kristen O., M.K Patterson. Thanks for loving the unpolished version of Heart but also telling me what I needed to hear in order to let this villain shine.

Maria Spada, for yet another kickass cover!

Katie Wolf, my editor, for your constant support, hours of hard work, and for loving my characters even in their crappiest forms.

And last, but never least, my readers. Without you, I wouldn't be able to do this. I can't wait to see where we go together! I hope Tolevarre feels like home when you need to escape, because it's been mine for two whole years now. Thank you for allowing me to live out my wildest dream. I love you all more than you'll ever know!

# ABOUT THE AUTHOR

Dany is an adult romantasy author currently living in southwest Michigan with her husband and four fur babies. Revenge of the Forgotten was her debut, introducing the world to Tolevarre and the bonded. Whenever she's not stuck in a fictional world, she enjoys traveling, diving into books that make her cry, and belting songs anywhere she goes like it's her own concert. She's known for her mid-scene cliffhangers and emotional twists with a side of comedy to lighten the blow.

INSTAGRAM: @DANYCROOKSAUTHOR
WEBSITE: WWW.DANYCROOKS.COM

# Also by Dany Crooks

Romantasy:

Revenge of the Forgotten (Cursed Gods Series Book 1)

Vengeance of the Gods (Cursed Gods Series Book 2)

Rom-Com:

Make Me Laugh (The Headliners Duology Book 1)

Coming soon!

Join my newsletter to get the inside scoop about
what's going on in the Dany Crooks Multiverse.